THE V CARD

LAUREN BLAKELY

LILI VALENTE

THE V CARD

By Lauren Blakely
and Lili Valente

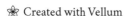

The Real Deal (Summer 2018)

Far Too Tempting

21 Stolen Kisses

Playing With Her Heart

Out of Bounds

The Caught Up in Love Series

Caught Up In Us

Pretending He's Mine

Trophy Husband

Stars in Their Eyes

The No Regrets Series

The Thrill of It

The Start of Us

Every Second With You

The Seductive Nights Series

First Night (Julia and Clay, prequel novella)

Night After Night (Julia and Clay, book one)

After This Night (Julia and Clay, book two)

One More Night (Julia and Clay, book three)

A Wildly Seductive Night (Julia and Clay novella, book 3.5)

Nights With Him (A standalone novel about Michelle and Jack)

Forbidden Nights (A standalone novel about Nate and Casey)

The Sinful Nights Series

Sweet Sinful Nights

Sinful Desire

Sinful Longing

Sinful Love

The Fighting Fire Series

Burn For Me (Smith and Jamie)

Melt for Him (Megan and Becker)

Consumed By You (Travis and Cara)

The Jewel Series

A two-book sexy contemporary romance series

The Sapphire Affair

The Sapphire Heist

ALSO BY LILI VALENTE

The Baby Maker (February 2018)

The Bad Motherpuckers Series (Standalones)

Hot as Puck

Sexy Motherpucker

Puck-Aholic

Puck me Baby

Sexy Flirty Dirty Romantic Comedies (Standalones)

Magnificent Bastard

Spectacular Rascal

Incredible You

Meant for You

The Master Me Series

(Red HOT erotic Standalone novellas)

Snowbound with the Billionaire

Snowed in with the Boss

Masquerade with the Master

Bought by the Billionaire Series

(HOT novellas, must be read in order)

Dark Domination

Deep Domination

Desperate Domination

Divine Domination

Kidnapped by the Billionaire Series

(HOT novellas, must be read in order)

Filthy Wicked Love

Crazy Beautiful Love

One More Shameless Night

Under His Command Series

(HOT novellas, must be read in order)

Controlling her Pleasure

Commanding her Trust

Claiming her Heart

To the Bone Series

(Sexy Romantic Suspense, must be read in order)

A Love so Dangerous

A Love so Deadly

A Love so Deep

Run with Me Series

(Emotional New Adult Romantic Suspense.

Must be read in order.)

Run with Me

Fight for You

The Bad Boy's Temptation Series

(Must be read in order)

The Bad Boy's Temptation

The Bad Boy's Seduction

The Bad Boy's Redemption

The Lonesome Point Series

(Sexy Cowboys written with Jessie Evans)

Leather and Lace

Saddles and Sin

Diamonds and Dust

12 Dates of Christmas

Glitter and Grit

Sunny with a Chance of True Love

Chaps and Chance

Ropes and Revenge

8 Second Angel

ABOUT THE BOOK

When you think about how easy it is to lose keys, phones, sunglasses, and your dignity on social media, you might figure it'd be a cinch for me to ditch my V Card.

You'd be wrong.

At 25, I run a successful business, live in a fantastic apartment, and have fabulous friends to go out with any night of the week. And yet I'm still a card-carrying member of a club I don't want to belong to anymore. Good thing I know just the man for the deflowering job —my brother's business partner and best friend.

Graham Campbell is charming, smart, and, I'm told, oh-so-skilled in the sack. As long as I keep my eyes on the prize, there's no way this pluck-the-flower project could possibly complicate matters.

* * *

Work and pleasure. As the CEO of a fast-growing company, I've been enjoying both to the fullest. What do I do when the board throws me for an unexpected loop so I can keep my business in my hands? I enlist the help of my best friend's little sister since she holds a big stake in the company. But then I learn there's another big stake she wants.

The one between my legs.

I can do this. Seven nights to teach her everything I know in the bedroom. There's no way I'll fall for her, even though she's earning top grades in every single sinfully sexy lesson. And turns out I'm learning something too. The trouble is I don't have the answer key to what to do when I fall hard for her.

And that throws a whole new hitch in my plans.

AUTHORS' NOTE

Once upon a time, a few years ago, two writer friends created an erotic, romantic suspense serial under the pen name Sophie Holloway. At its heart, that serial was the story of a woman asking her deceased brother's best friend to give her lessons in seduction. Recently, those same two writers started from scratch with that romantic concept and wrote an entirely new take on it as a fun, fresh, sexy romantic comedy. *The V Card* is that story, and it has been completely rewritten, from chapter one all the way through to the epilogue, as a brand-new lessons in seduction romance. Sophie's erotic serial is no longer available.

CHAPTER 1

GRAHAM

*J*ulie Andrews twirls in a field of flowers, her arms spread wide like she's going to hug the world, while the Alps rise majestically behind her.

"That's the one." I point to the light-blue T-shirt with the caption—*Look at all the fucks I give!*—scrawled in cursive above the famous image from *The Sound of Music.*

It's the perfect T-shirt for CJ.

One, she loves musicals.

Two, I'm always telling her she needs to give far fewer fucks. Shake off the little things. Don't sweat the small stuff.

Hell, look at me. I give so few fucks I'm practically a Zen master.

Although, for the record, the fucks I *do* give result in pure pleasure for the giver and the receiver.

"Would you like me to model that for you?"

I blink up at the unexpected offer. The curvy saleswoman bats her eyelashes suggestively. "It looks like it might be just my size," she says, those baby blues drifting down to where she wants me to look.

Holy hell. That's an eyeful. But of course, I'm only noticing her impressive rack because I want to get a look at her name tag. Ahem . . .

Olive.

I scrub a hand across my jaw. Damn, this shirt would look *excellent* on Olive.

Just have her try it on, the naughty devil on my shoulder whispers, determined to knock me off the wagon.

But that's not happening. Not today, or any day in the near future.

I fish a fifty from my wallet and set it on the counter, calling on my best Bruce Willis in *Die Hard 2. Just the fax, ma'am*. Damn, he was cool in that film. In every film.

"Just the shirt, ma'am," I say, flashing her a lopsided grin that has, admittedly, been known to melt panties.

"Ma'am?" She giggles. "You're making me feel old."

I swallow the teasing response on the tip of my tongue and slam on the charm brakes. Must. Stop. Flirting. I'm on the straight and narrow now. No distractions. Just laser-focus, like Bruce Willis disarming terrorists and saving Christmas.

"And can you wrap it up, please?" I ask, since CJ deserves the best. I can't just waltz into brunch, ask her to pretty please with sugar on top help me save my company, and hand her a T-shirt in a plastic bag. *Pfft.*

The least I can do is gift wrap my request. Besides, I pride myself on excellence in gift-giving.

I check the scores for the Portland Badgers, my favorite hockey team, as busty Olive who I'm *not* going to hit on—*not going to hit on, not going to hit on*—wraps soft pink paper around the shirt, tying it with a silky white bow before slipping it into a pink gift bag. Perfect for a woman like CJ. Pink is her color.

I thank Olive and head out of the boutique, the midmorning sun of a gorgeous spring day in Manhattan shining brightly above.

My driver, Gary, waits for me at the curb of this cobbled street in the Village, and I remind myself to give him an even bigger tip, since he never idles. The dude always turns off the engine while he waits for me, treating the earth right.

That's worth every penny of a tip.

Another thing worth every penny is having a town car at my disposal.

New York can suck it without a driver.

I can't believe there was a day when I didn't have this. Growing up with jack shit, my shoes held together by duct tape, I was lucky to have bus fare. I won't ever forget how lucky I am to have all *this* now, and to take care of my family, too, so their shoes are whatever kind they want.

I slide onto the cool leather seat, and my phone dings with a note from my good friend Luna, thanking me for recommending she see the newest Zach Galifianakis flick. Apparently, she laughed all the way through. I'm sending a quick *you're always welcome*, when another text lands. This one is from Lucy.

My shoulders tense, and I tell Gary to head to Ruby's

Kitchen on the Upper West Side, a farm-to-table place that has the best eggs in the city.

"Of course, Graham. Did you find what you were looking for?"

"I did. A perfect gift for CJ." A smile crosses my lips as I think of CJ and her nerdy addiction to novelty T-shirts, but the grin erases itself when I glance back down at my phone.

Lucy. Lush, but loony Lucy.

I really should block her number.

But if I did that, she would show up on my doorstep, crazy leaking out of every pore, and I would need a damned crowbar to pry her off of me. Briefly, I wonder what Bruce's John McClane would do in a situation like this, but then decide he wouldn't let it happen in the first place.

Just the fax, ma'am, and yippee-ki-yay-motherfucker.

LUCY: Hey there, G-Man. What are you up to?

I ROLL my eyes at the nickname I can't stomach then fire off a quick reply.

Busy.

Nothing shuts down a textual flirt attempt like a one-word reply. I'll just keep *Die Hard*ing it through the day, like John McClane would if he were the badass CEO of a sexy-as-sin lingerie company.

I delete the text and shove the phone into the pocket of my jeans.

Ex-girlfriends have a way of coming out of the

woodwork at the least opportune times, proving my long-standing belief that any relationship that lasts for more than a few weeks is a Big Mistake. Gigantic with a capital G.

Lucy, for all her sexy curves, filthy mouth, and willingness to tackle any challenge in the book on exotic sex positions, is proving to be the biggest mistake of them all.

The trouble is, I've always been a sucker for the crazy ones. They're just really good in bed.

Okay, fine, that's a lie.

I'm a sucker for all the ladies. Blond, brunette, redhead. Crazy, sane, smart. I love women. We've had a solid mutual appreciation society going on for years.

Until Lucy came along, and the focus-sucking vortex of her growing obsession with me served as a stark reminder that I don't have time for distractions in any shape or form. I don't have a minute to spare on a romantic relationship. Not with my business at stake. My industry is in a massive state of flux, and I need to concentrate on keeping the company train rattling along at full speed.

That's why I'm seeing CJ.

She's my secret weapon, the key to making sure Adored moves in the right direction, despite the suitors waiting in the wings for my baby, doing their best to tempt my shareholders.

Absently, I run my hand over the silky bow, frowning as my fingers slide across a card. Plucking it from the bag, I turn it over—*In case you change your mind about wanting more than the shirt.*

I smirk. So Olive found a way to get her number into my hands after all.

But I'm a good boy and have been since things ended with Lucy a few months ago.

A very good boy, who has no use for a beautiful woman's phone number.

Though a quickie *would* take my mind off of this upcoming board meeting, and Olive did seem like the kind of woman who would be fine with a one-night stand—flirty, but not raring to sink her claws into me . . .

I grab my phone again and tap out a message to Olive.

GRAHAM: Anything in particular you think would change my mind?

Almost immediately, my phone pings again.

My eyes practically pop out of my head when I open the multimedia message. Olive is one bold woman. One bold, busty woman.

I blow out a long stream of air, reminding myself I need to stay strong.

I type out a reply.

GRAHAM: Sorry, Olive. I sent that message as a mistake.

BEFORE I CAN HIT SEND, though, she replies again.

With a dozen smiley panda emoticons.

I groan, sliding a hand over my face.

Emoticons. Why did it have to be emoticons? Is it possible for anyone these days to communicate without a stupid smiley face?

My phone dings once more.

A winking emoticon.

Then a red-thong-wearing emoticon.

And finally, a unicorn jumping over an eggplant.

Fuck. This is what happens when I let myself even *think* about stepping off the straight, narrow, and celibate path.

GRAHAM: Sorry, Olive. I'm not the eggplant you're looking for. I need to delete your number.

THEN I DO.

I draw a deep breath and recommit myself to my one-step program.

The first and only step is this: *Resist engaging with the female of the species.*

Resist at any cost.

CHAPTER 2

GRAHAM

*S*kyscrapers slide by as the town car weaves its way up the avenue toward the Upper West Side. As Midtown's high-rises give way to brownstones and brick residential buildings, I recover my center and my focus.

Thankfully, I won't have to worry about Project Resistance with CJ.

CJ is like a little sister to me. Since her brother passed away, I've stepped into the protector role Sean filled so well. The past two years without my best friend and business partner haven't been easy, but being there for CJ has given me something to do, assuaging my anger and sadness. Every time I get pissed that a texting driver took my friend away, I think of something nice to do for CJ. It's a coping mechanism that works, and it's a hell of a lot less complicated than a booty call to the woman of the moment.

Gary pulls up outside Ruby's Kitchen, where CJ is already waiting on the curb, and my stress level drops another degree. She wears a sunshine-colored dress with strappy sandals and a jacket slung over her arm. Her chestnut hair curls softly in the spring breeze, and her nose is buried in her e-reader, as usual. The woman is an unrepentant bookworm, obsessed with horror novels that are every bit as scary as she is sweet.

"Weirdo," I mutter affectionately as I savor the sight of her, one of the few people in the world I can trust not to make life unnecessarily complicated. CJ shuts the cover on her e-reader as I swing out of the car.

"And he appears." She taps her foot playfully as I join her on the sidewalk. She tosses her dark hair off her shoulders as her face melts into that kid-in-a-candy-shop grin she's never outgrown.

That's one of the many things I adore about her. Her absolute fucking sweetness.

"I've been known to make appearances from time to time." I lean in to give her a chaste kiss on the cheek, enjoying the familiar jasmine scent of her hair.

"I'm assuming your tardiness means you had a most excellent night," she says, raising her eyebrows.

That's the thing about girls who have known you for more than a decade. They're well aware of your foibles and shortcomings, your strengths and your weaknesses.

"No way." I hold up two fingers. "Scout's honor. I was a good boy last night. I was only late because I saw something in a shop window I couldn't resist." I hold out the gift bag. "For you."

"Oh, stop," she says, smacking my chest. "You're making it impossible for me to be mad at you."

I smile. "You weren't mad at me, anyway. I gave you an excuse to read for an extra ten minutes."

"You speak the truth." She smirks as she reaches inside the bag with a soft coo at the sight of the paper. "Oh, it's beautiful."

Laughing, I say, "It's just wrapping paper."

She looks up and stares pointedly at me. "It's *not* just wrapping paper. It's a sign of thoughtfulness. The last guy I went on a date with brought me a candle his mother gave him three Christmases ago, said I'd look great by candlelight, and suggested we skip the movie and go get naked at his place."

I recoil. "What?"

"Little did he know that if he had *wrapped* that candle, I might have said yes," she says, a twinkle of mischief in her big brown eyes.

Red billows from my ears. Smoke comes out my eyes. The thought of CJ going home with this candle asshole boils my blood.

"You're joking," I grit out.

She cracks up and points at me. "Gotcha. Anyway. It's incredibly sweet of you to bring me a gift." She opens the bag, handing me the paper as she unfolds the shirt and laughs. "Graham, thank you! This is adorable. And way too naughty for casual Friday."

"Good thing there's life outside the office. For some of us, anyway."

"Hey, I'm out of the office now, aren't I?" She tucks her tee back in the bag, and nods toward the restaurant. "Shall we?"

"We shall," I say, my smile fading as I follow her to the hostess stand and then on through the throng of late-brunch-eaters to a table in the back courtyard.

As we settle in, the busboy brings the waters, and I

cut to the chase. "So, I hate to crash the Sunday Funday vibe, but I invited you to brunch with an ulterior motive. I need a favor."

She spreads her napkin on her lap with a raised brow. "What kind of favor?"

"I need you at next Monday's board meeting. As you know, we lost an important account last month when Beaux Rêves in Paris went with a cheaper option. Obviously, they aren't our only account, not by a long shot. But given how volatile the industry has been lately, I need to make it crystal clear to the shareholders that selling isn't the right path. With the number of mergers and acquisitions going on, they're seeing dollar signs, but quick money isn't the answer. That's where you come in."

"You want them to hear from me because of my shares?" she asks, her brow furrowing. "We don't have anything close to a majority."

Though CJ inherited Sean's share of the business when he passed away, that's not why I need her at the meeting. CJ has a way of putting people at ease, of winning their trust and confidence. She's a successful business owner in her own right—her accessories company Love Cycle Creations is growing by leaps and bounds every year. Plus, she was courted early on by an accessories conglomerate and she declined—totally the right call, as her company is now a rising star in her field.

I nod. "Of course, but that's not the only reason. I need to convince them that now is not the time to explore getting into bed with a huge multinational retailer. And to do that, it'll help to hear from someone with an insider's stock holdings and an outsider's perspective. I want them to hear from *you* in particular since you went through something so similar with Love Cycle."

"On a much smaller scale, though. My company is tiny compared to Adored."

"Size doesn't matter." I pause to wiggle an eyebrow for effect. "Well, in this case."

A faint blush spreads on her cheeks. "You and the innuendo."

"I do love innuendo. I also love Adored. That's why I want to keep it the way it is—growing, profitable, and independent. I don't want it swallowed whole by some faceless corporate giant." A smile teases her lips for a moment then disappears. I can't read her at all, so I'm on the edge of my seat, waiting for an answer. "Please, CJ," I add when she stays silent for a long beat. "I need you."

"You need me," she echoes, her brow smoothing as she sighs. She takes a drink of water, sets down her glass, and runs the tip of her tongue across her lips.

I watch her tongue move, wondering why I've never noticed how amazing her mouth is. She has the bee-stung lips of a cover girl, in a shade of pink so deep it brings to mind flushed, hot, intimate things.

Things I shouldn't be thinking of in her presence.

In *anyone's* presence.

Resist, Campbell, resist . . .

Finally, just as I'm gearing up to beg, she looks up, a mysterious smile curving her lips. "I know exactly what you need, Graham."

Damn, that sounded . . . naughty.

I reach for my water glass, needing something to cool me down since innocent words from a woman I've known forever are sending my thoughts straight into the gutter.

"But before I agree to your request," she adds, her fingers drumming lightly on the white tablecloth, "I need something from you, too. Something I've been thinking *long and hard* about. Very long. And very hard." Her eyes meet mine, trouble flickering in her gaze.

Glass halfway to my lips, I freeze.

Christ. Who the hell is this sexy-as-sin woman, and what has she done with CJ?

CHAPTER 3

CJ

Are you really going to do this? Really? For real? A voice inside my head keeps squeaking, but I ignore that wimpy coward because this is GO time.

This is the real deal.

This is do-or-die.

The stars are aligning, and the universe has given me the big thumbs-up for Operation V Card. You might not think it would be that hard for a reasonably attractive woman who isn't overly needy, smelly, or allergic to showers to lose her virginity, but you'd be wrong. I've been trying to get rid of this albatross hanging around my neck for years, but I'm looking down the barrel of age twenty-six with no acceptable de-flower-er in sight.

At least, not until now . . .

Now, Graham needs something from me—something that I'm happy to give because I've always believed in his vision for his company—and I need something from him. Things couldn't be going more perfectly if I'd scripted this brunch chat.

And sure, it's going to be weird, but it's *always* been weird between Graham and me. Graham, who I've lusted after since before I really knew what lust was. Even when I first laid eyes on him, back when he was seventeen and Sean's best friend, he was *all man*—broad shoulders, narrow waist, stubble-lined jaw, and a deep, husky voice that sent shivers down my spine. He ignited all my preteen fantasies. I daydreamed about Graham giving me my first kiss behind the pool house almost as often as I daydreamed about winning a road race cycling medal at the Summer Olympics.

At eleven, kisses and personal achievements comfortably coexist. At twenty-five, it's so much harder, especially in a city like New York, where everyone under the age of thirty is obsessed with success.

Professional success, *not* personal relationship success. No one wants to fall in love before thirty-five anymore, and even sex is something guys seem to want to pick up at a drive-through window. Or, better yet, have delivered by an Uber driver—sex and a side of cheesy fries from the diner down the block, please and thank you.

If I wait around to find the perfect guy on a dating app or at happy hour in the Meatpacking District, I'm going to be the world's oldest living virgin, and that is *not* a title I'm interested in holding.

Yes. All in. No backing out now. I flip my hair over my shoulder and straighten my spine. Graham's gaze flicks down to my chest before darting just as quickly back to my eyes.

Oh my God, Graham just looked at my boobs! Aha!

This is going to work! It's really going to work! Thank you, sexy yellow dress!

But when he speaks, his voice is cooler than it was before. "Oh, yeah? What exactly have you been thinking long and hard about, Ceej?"

I take a deep breath, blurting it out before I lose my courage, "I've been thinking about asking you to teach me things. Personal things."

He stares blankly, and for a moment I'm not sure he heard me. He brings his water to his lips and drinks again. "Teach you personal things like . . .?"

I sit tall, even as I twist my cloth napkin in circles in my lap. "You might think it's easy to date in this city, but it's not. At all."

"Oh, I know it's not easy." Graham rolls his eyes, proving he at least sort of gets where I'm coming from. "It's a minefield out there."

"Yes, it is!" I agree, nodding a little too fast. "A mine-field, and I know I'm going to step on a bomb sooner or later. But I don't want to step on just any bomb, you know what I mean? I want it to be a nice bomb. A, um . . . skilled bomb, who knows how to bomb effectively."

The metaphor isn't working. Graham looks more confused with every passing moment, and the waiter is circling behind him like a bird of prey ready to swoop down and snatch our menus, and this opportunity, from my hands.

I have to act now, before it's too late.

"This is the thing." I lift my hands, fingers spread wide, showing him I have nothing to hide. I'm putting it all out there and hoping he'll have mercy on me. "When

Dad moved to Greece with Betty after I finished college, Sean was so hyper protective that men were too scared to set foot on my doorstep. No lie. And then Sean died, and I was so sad I didn't care about dating for a long time."

Graham's gaze softens. "I know. I'm sorry."

I shake my head. "I don't want you to be sorry. I just want . . ." I swallow hard. "I want to move on. I want to be a normal twenty-five-year-old woman, but I feel like I'm so far behind I'll never catch up, you know? I'm drowning in all the things I don't know. So I just need . . . I need you to teach me about . . . about . . ."

About sex! Just say it, CJ!

Sex, intercourse, coitus, banging, the horizontal hula, the bow-chicka-wow-wow.

Woodenly, I erupt with, "Nookie."

Graham stares at me, his eyes wide and unreadable for one beat—two, three—while my heart crawls into my throat and puffs up like a blowfish.

Oh God, I've ruined everything. He's going to tell me I'm insane. He's going to tell me that the thought of me in a sexual situation makes him nauseous, and I'm going to feel like a fool for every single flirty thing I said to him. I never should have led with the long and hard bit. I shouldn't have tried to make this funny or cute—I should have just laid out my proposal with a calm voice and a level head, ensuring I could walk away with my chin up if he said "no, thanks."

I expect him to bolt for the door any second.

Instead, he puts his glass down, hitting the edge of the table and sloshing water onto the gravel beside us, earning a dirty look from the busgirl tidying up at a nearby table.

He clears his throat as he rights the glass, pulling at the collar of his shirt. "I'm sorry. What did you say?"

"I said 'nookie,'" I repeat, my cheeks still burning. "But, you know, use your own word. I'm open."

"You're open," he echoes, still sounding vaguely strangled, though he's unbuttoned the top button on his shirt. "Open to what exactly?"

"Graham, I'm twenty-five, and I spend most nights at home watching television or at the gym riding a bike that's going nowhere," I confess, embarrassed, though this isn't news to him. He knows I'm practically a nun. He teases me about it often enough. "I want more than that. I want an adult relationship, but other adults don't want *me*."

"You're crazy. I—"

"I'm not crazy. I'm inexperienced, and the real grown-ups can sense that, and it scares them away. That leaves me with the weird candle guys and the losers looking for a meaningless hookup." He starts to interrupt me, but I barrel on. "I want more than that. But I don't have the skills to seal the deal, and at this rate, I'm never going to get them unless I go to drastic measures to catch up. Do you understand what I'm saying?"

"I think so." A flush creeps up Graham's neck as he shakes his head. "But you can't seriously be saying you want me to . . ."

His gaze drops to my breasts again, lingering long enough on the place where my dress gives way to skin that it gives me the strength to nod and murmur, "Yes, that's exactly what I'm saying."

He swallows hard, looking over one shoulder and then the other before turning back to me with a harsh whisper, "Sean would cut my dick off. Not to mention the fact that you and I—" He motions between us with a swift jerk of his hand. "We're friends, CJ. Just friends. I don't think of you like that."

"And that's fine," I say, forcing a smile. "You don't have to think of me as anything but a friend. And a student. I'll be a good student, I promise. I'm a fast learner. Especially when I'm invested in the subject matter."

Graham's eyes lift to the blue sky overhead as he mumbles something that sounds like a prayer for strength.

I sigh, my hope fading. But this is my one shot at getting what I need from the only man left in the world I trust, and I'm not going to give up so easily. Just because I'm a virgin, doesn't mean I'm inexperienced in other areas, like speaking my mind or campaigning for my goals. And, like a good businesswoman, I plan on keeping this deal with Graham on the transactional level. Sure, I've lusted after the man. He's as handsome as anything, and a total softie beneath his occasionally gruff exterior.

None of that matters in this situation, however. I'm focused, determined, and completely able to separate my heart from my head, just like I have to do at work when juggling my roles as friend and boss.

That's what I'll do if he says yes.

I *must* convince him to say yes.

"Graham, I'm sick of feeling like a fish on a bicycle every time I'm in mixed company. Sure, men check me out, but as soon as they realize I have no idea how to flirt, let alone anything else, their interest fades pretty quickly." I keep my head up, refusing to feel ashamed. "For once, I want to feel sexy. Like I know what I want and I know how to get it. I thought you, of all people, would understand that."

Graham sighs. "CJ, you're an intelligent, successful woman. And you're a fucking knockout."

He thinks I'm a knockout? He's never said anything like that before. Never. Not even last New Year's Eve when I wore my red cleavage dress to the Adored holiday party.

"You could have any man you want," he continues, proving he hasn't been listening. "You don't need me. And you don't want me, trust me."

With my eyes fixed on his, I lean in until our faces are only a few inches apart, and I play my ace. "But I do want you, Graham. I've heard the rumors. You may not be aware of it, but your ex-girlfriends talk. A lot. And they have nothing but good things to say." I pause, arching a meaningful brow. "About *everything*."

His eyes glitter. "I'm far from the only man in the city with that kind of reputation."

"True. But you're the only one who's my friend." I lace my fingers together as I add, "I trust you, Graham. I know you won't hurt me or take advantage of me or make me feel like a fool if I don't get it all right straight out of the gate. You're the only one I can ask a favor like this."

He frowns, but I can see him weakening. "What exactly are we talking about? What do you want me to teach you?"

"Well, the exact lesson plan is up to you." I shrug one shoulder, playing it casual so I won't scare him away. "But I would like it to be thorough. I want to be well-versed in all areas."

He starts to look shell-shocked again. "All areas?"

"Yes. Well, you know. Oral. That's a must. And all the normal stuff. But I'd also like to branch out. Be a little adventurous, you know? Maybe some role-playing or light bondage if things are going well—that sort of thing." I shrug again, fighting to suppress a nervous giggle. I've never said most of those things aloud before, let alone asked a guy to help me do them. In the interest of keeping my cool, I conclude with, "I just want to be able to drive a man crazy. To please and satisfy him in every way."

Graham moves his napkin from his lap to the table.

Swallows.

Clears his throat.

He clears his throat again as he crosses his arms at his chest.

"And I should probably mention that I'm a virgin," I blurt, figuring it's better to get it all out up front so he knows the deep water he's thinking about wading into.

His eyes bulge in response, but I'm ready for him. This isn't the first time I've shocked and appalled someone with my ancient V card.

"I know." I lift my hands at my sides, my palms facing Graham. "It's unusual. I get it, but going to an all-girls college was not conducive to losing my virginity. At all. Add in the fact that I lived with my brother when I first moved to Manhattan, and everything that happened after, and the stars did not align. And now that I've started dating again, well . . . I feel a bit radioactive. Men are a lot weirder about sleeping with virgins than you would think."

Graham's expression is an eloquent mixture of amusement, horror, and disbelief that would be funny if I wasn't feeling like I just flashed my underwear in church. I can't remember the last time I felt so completely exposed, all my secrets and hopes twisting in the wind, waiting to see what Graham will decide to do with them.

After a long, silent moment, he grunts.

Once. One grunt.

"So, is that one grunt for a no?" I ask, brows lifting. "Or one for a yes?"

His blue eyes blaze at me, shining with . . . something new. Something dark and delicious that makes my skin heat and a series of delicious and slightly terrifying tingles dance from my lips to the tips of my toes and back again.

He shakes his head. "I couldn't, even if I thought it was a good idea—which I don't. I'm on a sabbatical."

I frown. "A sabbatical? From . . . sex?"

"Yep," he says, a smirk curving his lips. "A sex-batical."

"Why would you do that?"

"Excessive emoji use for one."

"That makes you monk it up?"

He nods. "But more than that, sex complicates things, and I need to be zeroed in on business. It's all work and no women until I calm the skittish shareholders. I'm all about Adored right now. I made a promise to myself, and I don't break my promises."

"I see," I say, my eyes narrowing on his as I decide to play dirty. "But I'm not really a woman. I'm just CJ, your friend and a shareholder you need to back you up at the next board meeting, right?"

"Caroline Jessica," Graham says, my full name a warning. "You wouldn't . . ."

"Oh, but I would." I smile sweetly. "So, my friend, in exchange for one week of sexual education, I will do whatever you want me to do next Monday. I'll tap-dance on the boardroom table if you think that's necessary. Though, for the record, I believe in your vision for Adored and that you're the only person qualified to lead the company. And I will express that eloquently to the board . . . assuming you agree to play ball."

"Christ . . ." Graham's eyes close as his fingers come to rub his temples.

"Think it over, and let me know." I stand, picking up my clutch and gift bag. We haven't eaten—hell, we haven't even ordered—but there's no way I'm going to be able to sit across the table from Graham and force down food after a conversation like this one.

It's time to make my exit and hope I'm leaving with the upper hand.

I pause at the door leading out of the patio to wave goodbye and find Graham watching me with that new, not-entirely-safe look in his eyes again, and I shiver.

Part of the shiver is fear. What if this ruins things between us? Sure, I have other friends, but no one I've known as long or cared about as much as Graham. What if he says no and decides never to talk to me again?

Then another voice in my head whispers, *And what if he says yes? Are you ready for that, Caroline Jessica Murphy?*

But as I flee the restaurant and head out onto Amsterdam Avenue, the electrified feeling lifting the hair at the back of my neck has nothing to do with fear, and everything to do with possibility.

CHAPTER 4

GRAHAM

*W*hat. The. Hell?

I rub my finger against my ear as I wander through Central Park in a daze an hour later.

Maybe I've slipped into an alternate reality, like in *Fight Club*, only I'm now playing the part of a sex tutor after-hours. And the first rule of Sex Club? When the woman you're supposed to look out for like a little sister propositions you, SAY NO.

Right?

How can I possibly say yes?

My job is to scowl at potential suitors, to tell her no one is good enough for her, and to make it clear she should never settle for some schmuck who regifts candles to lubricate the path to sex.

You would lubricate the path in a much classier fucking way . . .

And Devil Graham is back in a big way.

She needs you. You're the only man for the job.

No, Devil Graham, you are wrong. I can't be the guy

who looks out for her during the day, and her sex tutor at night.

Look how well those split roles worked for the narrator in *Fight Club*. I would rather stay out of the mental ward, thank you very much.

"Get out of the way, Wall Street."

I snap my gaze up as a speed-demon jogger tears by, barking at me. Huh. Apparently, I'm walking in the fast lane on the running path. Well, excuse the hell out of me.

I raise a hand in a mock-friendly wave, calling out, "No problem, man. I'll just be the guy passing you tomorrow."

But I don't run in Central Park. I'm a Hudson River Greenway guy. Besides, wearing a button-down shirt doesn't make me look like a Wall Street douchebag. I'm just a guy dressed nicely for brunch with a friend I've known since she was a kid, who wants me to teach her sex tricks.

As I walk east across the Great Lawn, I try again to make sense of CJ's desire to learn how to please a man. Something is off with that. It should be the other way around. Some lucky bastard should be busting his ass— and everything else—to please *her*.

My dick insists he and I could teach her how a real man treats a woman. But my dick isn't the best barometer. Dicks are notoriously untrustworthy. A dick knows one thing—it wants to go home. All the time. Home being the promised land between a woman's soft, welcoming thighs.

That's why I can't trust my dick to make this call, even though the prospect of sweet, funny, clever CJ asking me—no, begging me—to fuck her is a bigger turn-on than I would have imagined possible.

And that's the problem. I need to get my head in the game and put my libido on the sidelines. As I walk, I focus on the best boner-killer known to heterosexual man.

Another man.

Yep. Works like a charm.

Down-boy achieved in seconds as I think of Sean.

We were raised on the proverbial different sides of the tracks, but none of that mattered when we interned at the same company in high school. Hockey fans through and through, we connected over a shared devotion to the sport, as well as our drive to conquer the business world. Hell, we hatched the idea for our company back when we were dirty-minded teens. But we stuck with it, all through college and beyond, launching Adored and turning it into a success.

He guarded our company like a bear, watching over it with unwavering devotion.

He was like that with his sister, too. That was his style. He had the overprotective brother thing going in spades. Their mom died when they were both young, and when their dad moved to Greece, all roads to CJ's social life went through Sean. At six-foot-three, with a bruiser body and a gruff exterior, no one wanted to fuck with him. It's no surprise, I suppose, that she didn't date much in Manhattan—not when she was living down the hall from someone who could put the fear of God into other men with one look.

But even so, it's still messing with my head that she's a virgin. Like, a real virgin? Not just today's virgins, who consider themselves chaste if their ass hasn't been deflowered?

How could a woman as beautiful, outgoing, and fucking adorable as CJ be a card-carrying member of the V club at age twenty-five? CJ is the stuff erotic dreams are made of. And in those dirty dreams, I can picture leading her somewhere private and stripping off her blouse, kissing those luscious tits of hers, making her moan. I can imagine discovering the flavor of her kiss, making her gasp as my tongue sweeps across her soft skin for the first time.

A horse and carriage clomp by, the horse neighing.

Yeah, that's my cue to *whoa nelly* on my brain.

And to violate the first rule of Fight Club. The real rule.

I have to talk about this.

I need a reality check.

I need my good friend Luna, former business school study buddy and person I can always count on to give it to me straight—even when it hurts. And it just so happens she's not far away.

I head to her food truck, texting her that I'll be there in three minutes.

As I head up the cobblestone path not far from the carousel, she pops out of the doorway of the blue Luna's Sweets truck on the other side of the roundabout. "Hey there, stranger." Luna waves at me, smiling from behind her cat-eye glasses, her blond ponytail swishing in the breeze. "What are you doing here on a Sunday? Let me guess—you couldn't keep away from my whoopie pies."

I hold my arms out wide. "Who in the world can resist a whoopie pie?"

"No one. And let's keep it that way. We open in thirty minutes, and I want a line as far as the eye can see. But you can have one now." She winks and then slips back into the truck, returning a few seconds later with a whoopie pie in a paper boat. "For you, you closet pie junkie."

I pat my flat belly. "Shh. Don't tell anyone the real reason I run five miles every day is that I'm addicted to your whoopie." I hold up a hand. "Wait, that sounded filthy. Reboot."

Luna laughs. "It's okay. I'm used to your dirty mind. But thankfully, I'm immune to your charms."

"You wound me."

"I know. You've never recovered from me choosing team chick over team dick, have you?" She waits for my usual assurances that yes, having my only bisexual friend swear off cock for the rest of her life was the most traumatizing event of my graduate school experience.

But my brain is fuzzy, and I'm not ready to fire back with our usual repartee. She seems to sense it, her brows drawing together as she scans my face. "Wow, you look like shit. What's up?"

"You look lovely, too."

She punches my shoulder. "Shut up. I mean that with great affection."

I rub my shoulder, pretending she hurt me. "And I appreciate your affection, even the kind where you punch me." I take a deep breath and dive into the crazy end of the pool. "Ever feel like everything you thought you knew about the universe went up in smoke in a single morning?"

"Seeing as I barely understand how string theory supposedly ties the universe together, no. But I get what you're saying. Come on. Let's take a walk." She unties her apron, wadding it into a ball and tossing it to the teenager in the truck. "Hold the fort. I'll be back."

We head through the trees and into the shade, Luna wiggling her hands into the pockets of her oversize sweater. "Talk to me."

"It's CJ Murphy. You know, Sean's little sister?"

Luna hums thoughtfully. "Cute, curvy brunette at graduation? The one Sean treated like she was made of glass and made her go back to the hotel with their dad before we all went out for drinks?"

"Yes, that's the one," I say. "We've stayed close since Sean passed, and I, um . . . well, I learned something about her today." I take my time with this. A part of me thinks I shouldn't be sharing CJ's secret, but Luna is a vault. She keeps all my confidences, always has, and I can't process this new intel solo.

"She's an ax murderer in her spare time?" Luna quips.

"Ha. Funny. But you're not far off, oddity-wise." I take another bite, finishing the pie and taking a deep breath. "But listen, this is personal. So please don't share."

She gives me a you-can't-be-serious look. "As if."

"I mean it, Luna. You can't even tell Princess," I say, referring to Valerie, Luna's tall, strong, kick-ass-and-take-names wife. She's the head of ticket operations at Madison Square Garden, as well as a part-time karate instructor, and about as far from the princess stereotype as you can get, but it's sweet that Luna uses that nickname.

She frowns. "It better be important if you're asking me to keep it from Valerie. We don't do secrets—even other people's secrets."

I toss the pie boat in a trash can, stop in my tracks, and heave a sigh. "Yes, it's important, and I probably shouldn't breathe a word, but this is screwing with my head, and I need your help."

She taps her watch. "I hear you, Graham Cracker. And you know I'll help if I can. But I can't do anything until you spit it out."

"She's interested in going back to school," I blurt out.

Luna furrows her brow. "For what? Business? Doesn't she run her own company already?"

"Not that kind of school." I cut the bullshit, adding in a softer voice, "She wants *me* to be her teacher. Her one-on-one, private sex ed teacher."

Luna's mouth falls into an O. "Wow. I just can't picture . . ." She blinks behind her glasses. "She seemed so shy the one time I met her. She actually came out and said she wanted a sex tutor? Are you sure you under-stood her?"

I scoff. "Please. I earned an A-plus in that subject."

A sharp-eyed stare is my response.

"Trust me. There was no innuendo. No subtlety. She was one hundred percent direct. She wants me to develop a lesson plan in how to please a man. Appar-ently, she doesn't feel she's as well versed as she wants to be."

Luna snorts. "But no way she's a virgin, right? She's a

babe. Straight-up foxy. I mean, if I weren't madly in love with Princess, I'd do her."

I roll my eyes. "Good to know." Then I sidestep the virgin question because that's not my confidence to share. I don't have to reveal the full truth to get Luna's advice. "She's inexperienced. And she wants some . . . how shall we say, fine-tuning. I guess she feels in today's world, she needs a few tricks up her sleeve to hold her own on the battlefield."

"It is pretty crazy out there," Luna murmurs. "I thank God every day that I'm not single anymore. And well, I guess it's natural that she would ask you. You're her friend, and you have a reputation as a talented guide through hetero O-town, if you're into that kind of thing." She shrugs. "So, what did you say?"

"I didn't say anything. I mean, this is crazy, right?" I ask, shocked that Luna isn't immediately telling me to back away from my best friend's little sister. "I have to tell her no. Sean would have lost his fucking mind. I can't do that to him."

"Sean would have been happy if the poor girl ended up locked in a convent somewhere." Luna presses her lips together. "And Sean, rest his sweet, over-protective soul, isn't here to make this decision. CJ is, and you are. And if the woman needs and wants help, it's something to consider. Do *you* want to do it? To help someone you obviously care about?"

I shake my head because I can't go there.

But I also can't help but think of how CJ would respond to a kiss, my body pressing tight to hers. I can practically feel her curves against my chest, hear her calling my name in her husky voice.

Now that the idea has been planted, I can't get her out of my mind.

"But that's not the point," I say, clearing my throat. "The point is, I have to convince her to let this go, don't you think? She should flush the sex ed idea and stick to dating until she finds the right guy."

Luna laughs. "You're a dumbass, Graham," she says bluntly. "CJ knows what she wants, or she wouldn't have had the guts to ask for it. Besides . . ." She waves a hand at the city skyline rising like jagged gray teeth above the green trees of the park. "You've romanced and bestowed orgasms upon half the female population of the city. And now you have a chance to put all that experience to use for good."

I scoff. "Seriously? For good? That's how you see this?"

She nods vigorously. "Yes. You've been asked to help a friend. And if she doesn't get a yes from you, what makes you think a determined, bright woman like CJ isn't going to find someone else to teach her the ropes?"

My gut clenches at that thought. Someone else teaching her? Touching her?

"You really think she'd ask someone else?"

Luna shrugs. "Never underestimate the determination of a woman when it comes to getting what she needs. And for the record, if she played for my team, and she'd come to me before I was a married woman, damn straight I would have taught her how to float down the Lesbian River."

"I didn't realize it was a river," I say drily.

Luna wiggles her eyebrows in response. "Just think. What if she goes to a sexpert? Do they have those? If there are people who get paid to cuddle, surely there are sexperts? Guys who will teach CJ all the dirty deeds as long as she's willing to pay the right price . . ."

The thought is stomach-turning. I don't want her going to some sleazy sexpert, or even another friend.

I don't want her turning to anyone else. Period. Sex-batical or no sex-batical, that's unacceptable. And honestly, it's probably worth breaking my two-months-and-counting fast.

I raise my gaze heavenward. Sean's not here—may he rest in peace—but if his sister is fixated on finding someone in this city of millions to teach her how to come undone, and make a man do the same, it's going to be me.

And fuck, do I ever want to see her come.

Maybe that makes me a bad man, but I'm finding being good is rapidly losing its appeal.

I walk Luna back to her truck, hug her goodbye, and then open CJ's number on my phone.

I'm her friend, and I care deeply for her. I want her to know that. I also want to show her what kind of teacher I am.

The kind who doesn't settle for less than 100 percent from his student.

CHAPTER 5

CJ

I pedal harder. Faster. I'm climbing Mount Freaking Everest now. I'm cresting the icefall, then the Lhotse wall, and now heading to the summit. My heart hammers so hard it's like a drumbeat in my ears. My blood pumps rapid-river fast.

But not fast enough.

I push the tension higher on the bike. Set the incline steeper. Ride harder. My quads scream at me, and my lungs feel like they want to rip right out of my chest.

But "Don't Stop Me Now" by Queen blasts in my ears, nearly intense enough to drown out my thoughts.

Nearly.

But not enough.

Because no matter how hard I work out at the gym this afternoon, no matter how loudly I blast my favorite Retro Cycling Goodness playlist, I can't help but think I am a colossal idiot.

Who the heck asks a friend to take off their training wheels?

Correction. Who the heck asks a friend who isn't even *attracted* to her to pop her cherry? And then holds his company hostage?

I need to face-palm right now, but if I do I'll slide off the bike and crumple to a pathetic death on the sweaty floor of my gym wearing my *Good Grammar is Sexy* T-shirt, and all things considered, that's not how I want to go. The gym charges a fortune for towel rental so who knows how much they would charge for a full-body disposal.

As my heart slams against my rib cage, I imagine Graham poring over the newspaper on his tablet, quietly comparing the latest tragic world events to the tragedy of a woman reaching her mid-twenties without finding anyone willing to pluck her daisy. Graham out for a jog and running out of breath because he can't stop cracking up over silly CJ, the weirdo spinster virgin. Graham in the middle of a meal and losing his appetite as he realizes he'll have to find a gentle way to tell me that he has no interest in acquiring the deed to my property.

After all, it's been hours, and he hasn't called. He hasn't texted. He's clearly going to give me a big fat no and tell me to hit the road.

I raise my chin, try to inhale deeply, exhale completely, and let go.

It's cool. I'm chill. I'll just ride till I collapse, then I'll nap till the embarrassment washes away in, oh say, 2056.

My phone rattles on the control panel, startling me.

I slow my pace, nearly spinning off the bike when I see his name.

Graham . . .

My heart leaps into my throat.

This is it. The moment my brazen attitude slaps me in the face.

GRAHAM: Hey

I STUDY the text as if something, anything, in those three letters will tell me if that's a let's-get-it-on *hey* or a please-don't-throw-your-vagina-at-me *hey*. But I come up empty, so I serve it back to him.

CJ: Hey

GRAHAM: How's it going?

I'M HOT. Sweaty. Panting.

But of course *that* would send the wrong message. And the message I need to send right now is one of repentance and contrition. I need to let Graham know I'm sorry I crossed a line.

CJ: Oh you know . . . I rode this stationary bike to Brooklyn and back, uphill both ways, and basically bit my nails to the quick in an epic stress fest.

GRAHAM: You're not a nail-biter. Also, impressive cardio, Ceej.

CJ: You're right. I'm not normally a nail-biter. But I'm clearly not walking the straight and narrow path today. I've been worried that I overstepped and now you think I'm a crazy person . . .

GRAHAM: Not any crazier than I thought you were yesterday.

I GROAN as I tug my buds out of my ears. *Crazy.* He's confirmed that he thinks I'm crazy. I watch my sex ed plans go up in flames, fueled by the tinder of Graham's and my forever damaged relationship. Biting my lip, I text—

CJ: I ruined our friendship, didn't I?

GRAHAM: No. Of course not.

CJ: You're sure?

GRAHAM: I'm sure. I'm glad you were honest with me.

And that you trusted me enough to share something so personal.

CJ: Even though I held you hostage with my demands?

GRAHAM: You're a tough negotiator beneath that sweet exterior. But I've always known you were made of steel and sugar.

My lips press together. Steel and sugar. That's not necessarily a bad combo, is it?

GRAHAM: Seriously, you could never ruin our friendship. No matter what schemes you hatch up in your squirrel brain.

I WINCE, my stomach cratering. Embarrassment washes over me. My shoulders sag. He can deny it all he wants, but he clearly thinks I'm storing up psycho for the winter.

But before I can type something sufficiently relaxed-sounding to hide my shame, my phone pings again.

GRAHAM: Meet me at Patio West at nine p.m. tomorrow. Be ready for lesson one.

"HOLY SHIT," I murmur, hand coming to cover my

mouth. "Holy, holy, holy shit!" My hands are shaking so badly with excitement that it takes three tries to tap out my reply—*See you there*—and hit send.

Resisting the urge to thrust my arms into the air in a V for victory, I start pedaling, but inside I'm not cycling. I'm soaring, flying so high I can't wipe the stupid grin off my face or keep giddy laughter from bubbling at my lips.

I'm finally going to lose *it*, the one thing I for sure don't want to keep.

Goodbye, V card.

CHAPTER 6

GRAHAM

I am on fire today.

It's only ten, and I've already logged five miles on the Hudson River Greenway, solved a thorny supply issue with the production department halfway around the world, and answered all pressing emails from business partners.

That's what a good old-fashioned five a.m. alarm and the prospect of taking care of my other favorite kind of business after-hours has done for me.

Add in a breakfast meeting with my finance team at the Parker Meridien that went swimmingly, and I'd like to bottle this energy and take a hit whenever I'm losing focus.

I return to the office on Fifty-Sixth, stabbing the elevator button for the twenty-fifth floor and whistling a happy tune.

Eleven more hours till school starts.

I've never been more excited to go to class.

Then again, I've never been this kind of teacher, and

I have a feeling I'm going to enjoy every single second of tutoring CJ one-on-one.

As the elevator chugs upward, my phone buzzes with a text. I grab it quickly, in case it's CJ. But my jaw clenches when I see the name.

I mutter a curse, but then take a deep, fueling breath as I open Lucy's message. The last time I saw her, the day I broke things off, she'd asked if she could move in with me instead. Can you say whiplash? First, we'd been dating one month. No way did I want her to move in. Second, I wanted to *end* the relationship—that's what "this isn't working for me" means.

I brace myself for her note, hoping it's not another plane ticket to fly out of town with her, or some comment about what I was wearing on the running path the other morning, since I've noticed her a few times on the greenway when she was never a runner before.

LUCY: Thinking of you and that scarf you said you wanted to use on me.

I GIVE my phone the side-eye. What is she talking about? We never discussed a scarf, and I don't have time for mind games. But I can't just keep hoping she'll leave me the hell alone.

I need to send a very clear message.

GRAHAM: Please stop texting me. And don't attempt to contact me again.

I ERASE HER TEXT. I delete her contact info. Then I hit delete on Lucy's space in my brain.

Done.

Gone.

Washed clean.

While my messages are open, I tap out a quick note to my parents, asking if Mom wasted Dad on the tennis court again today. Her quick reply—*Of course. Three-love. Booyah!*—makes me smile. Their condo, their tennis lessons, the fun they're having after decades of killing themselves in dead-end jobs—that's why I've worked my ass off since I was a kid with my first paper route. Even on the day the bank kicked my family out of our house years ago, I knew the future was going to be brighter. Because I would make it brighter. I was determined to get out and make good for all of us.

And I did. My parents love their condo in West Palm Beach, and every day I'm glad I bought it for them before putting the down payment on my own NYC apartment.

The elevator dings, and the doors whoosh open on my floor, on the kingdom I built from the ground up. I say hello to the receptionist, then stride through the work space, flashing smiles and quick hellos to my team on the way to my corner office.

When I reach the door, a voice calls out. "Did you see that penalty last night?"

I swivel around, my eyes widening, my disgust over

the ridiculous penalty against my Portland Badgers returning in full force. "It was highway robbery," I say to Brian, a rising marketing star at the company and a rabid hockey fan, too.

He shakes his head, his blue eyes narrowing as he walks toward me. "I'm telling you, the refs hate our guys because we're too damn good."

"Oh, to be hated for being amazing. Something we should all aspire to." I glance at my watch. "Hey, you want to review the PowerPoint for next week?"

Marketing the new lines is critical to my plans for the company. In this fast-moving industry, we need to be spot-on with communicating to consumers. But in a sexy, delicious way.

"Absolutely. Let's make it amazing."

"Let's make it so damn good the board will be blown away," I agree.

"That's the only way to treat a board."

I push open the door for my office and let Brian head in first. He joined the company a few years ago, a newly minted MBA, and he's eager as a Boy Scout. He has a fresh-faced go-getter attitude as well as a tenacious work ethic that I dig.

We roll up our sleeves and tackle the presentation I need to make to the board next week, refining a few slides to make it even better. When we're done, I hold up a hand to high-five. "This is like a hat trick in the Stanley Cup Final."

"You know it," he says, laughing as he drags a hand through his brown hair.

But then I have to ask myself if it is.

It's almost there, but . . .

I lean back on my leather couch, thinking.

My mind snags on something from my emails earlier today. One of our partners wanted to see if they could move up the launch of a new line of candy-colored corsets in time for the fall, a pre-holiday push, but the marketing still feels a little off. *Have your cake and wear it, too* is a cute slogan for the collection, but every model we're using in the print campaign looks like she hasn't eaten cake in at least seven years. Maybe eight. I would prefer the marketing package hit an inclusive note, to embrace all body sizes and all women, be they stick thin or curvy and full-figured. We've built our high-end brand on that message and can't stray too far. Adored's brand mystique has to remain top-notch.

I share my thought process with Brian, and he nods his agreement. "With a reshoot and a few positioning adjustments, we might be able to pull this off," I say, a burst of excitement zipping through me, as it so often does when I feel the possibilities of what I can do in this business.

I started Adored for three reasons. One, I wanted to build a company I loved from the ground up, applying all my business acumen to the sole goal of making my venture so wildly successful that no one in my family would have to worry about money ever again.

I've checked that off.

Two, I fucking adore women, especially in lingerie, and particularly when lingerie is doing its job making them feel sexy and beautiful.

And three, I wanted to work with my best friend. We accomplished that, and part of me wants to fight to keep

Adored independent because of Sean. I know he would have wanted that, too.

This presentation on the new line will be key to getting the board excited about my vision for Adored, so they can see that selling out is not an option.

After we've finished laying out a plan for campaign adjustments and Brian leaves, I check the clock, pleased that it's now T-minus seven hours till launch. I'm ready to give myself an A-plus for kicking ass at the office today. Maybe women and work haven't been meshing for me lately, but hell, it sure seems that night school is better than an iced coffee for focus.

Note to self: if you ever change careers, consider being a sex tutor. It streamlines the focus and keeps your dick in the game.

As the clock ticks past three, I review the design for some new panties. Tilting my head, I study the way the lace skims high on the thighs of the model. How it slides between her legs. How there's just enough of a pattern to leave most of what's underneath to the imagination.

And my imagination goes to CJ.

What does she wear under those cute T-shirts? What does she sleep in? I'm imagining her in bed in her snug apartment in the Meatpacking District, sliding under the covers in a burgundy baby doll, dark against her pale skin. It'd ride up to her belly, revealing kissable flesh.

A barely audible groan escapes my throat. Thank fuck my door is closed because I'm staring at the screen as if it's the best porn reel around.

But it's not the panties on the screen that do it for me.

It's the movie in my mind.

I'm undressing CJ, discovering she wears a pale-blue push-up bra with flowers embroidered into it, the demi cups ensuring her tits spill over the tops. I'm seeing a pair of matching panties with delicate patterns and sheer lace.

In the lingerie business, you learn that every woman is an individual when it comes to her sensuality. Some want to lead with bold animal prints, others crave delicate flowers. Some love unapologetic, make-no-mistake-what's-on-my-mind black, while others covet bright, fiery red or soft, pale pink.

I know what I would like to see CJ in, but I also want to learn how she sees herself.

What does she slide on beneath her clothes to make her feel confident and beautiful? What brings out her seductive side? Has she even figured out the power of a well-chosen panty and bra set?

Maybe that's something I can help her with, too, and give myself something to look forward to in the process.

I pick up the phone and arrange for a special delivery.

CHAPTER 7

CJ

*T*his could be it. The night everything changes. The night I start the journey from Behind the Sex Curve to Head of the Fucking Class.

Assuming, of course, that the gift box Graham had sent to my apartment means what I think it means.

"Sexy panties in a fancy gift box mean exactly what you think they mean, genius," I murmur to my reflection in my compact as my cabbie whizzes down Sixth Avenue, weaving in and out of traffic in a way that would give me a heart attack if I made the mistake of looking out the window. "This is it. Time to get your head in the game and think positive, ready-to-pounce thoughts."

Oh God . . . ready-to-pounce thoughts.

I thought I was ready—I'm the one who put this kinky bargain on the table, for goodness sake—but now that my theory is about to become reality, I'm so nervous it feels like my tongue is trying to crawl down my throat and hide out in my stomach. I was expecting lesson one to be something tamer—a way to ease into this, like sinking into a pool of slightly too-hot water—but then there were panties.

And panties mean business.

"Let you out on this side?" the driver asks, motioning to the corner just ahead.

"Yes, th-that's fine." I fluff my hair, run my tongue over my front teeth, and snap my compact shut with a firm *click* before swiping my credit card and adding a healthy tip.

And then me, my black skirt that hits at the knees, and the black lace panties that reveal more of my butt than I'm pretty sure I've ever revealed to anyone are off to the races. The lace underwear isn't a thong, but it doesn't cover my cheeks, either. They cut halfway across my rear. Perhaps that means Graham is an ass man. The thought makes me simultaneously want to giggle and to hide my face behind my hands while I blush ruby red.

There's also an embroidered butterfly on the semi-sheer front, right at the top by my hipbone. If I'm trying to read his panty selection like a mug of tea leaves, I guess that means he thinks I'm a butterfly. Hopefully he's right, and I'm finally ready to emerge from my cocoon.

But I remind myself that I'm a business butterfly, and that breed keeps the heart separate from anything below the belt. I move faster down the street, shivering slightly at the chill in the night air, wrapping my arms around my silky pink blouse.

A few minutes later, after visiting the Starbucks bathroom a few doors down from the restaurant, because anxiety makes my microscopic bladder even more hyperactive, I'm stepping out of the elevator at Patio West.

Excessively well-dressed and on-trend people gather in cozy clusters around the deck, which is illuminated by antique gas lamps and humming space heaters scattered across the rooftop bar. At this hour, the sun is long down and the lights are turned low, but it's bright enough for me to spot Graham. I could pin-point him a mile away on a cloudy day with a bag over his head, based on his broad, take-no-prisoners shoulders alone.

But he's not here. There are no suitably-sized shoulders in attendance at the bar, or at any of the tables.

Doubt flashes through my chest for the thousandth time since my panty present arrived. What if Graham's changed his mind? What if the panties don't mean what I think they mean? What if he was on his way here and was in a horrible accident and is now in the hospital, fighting for his life, because I'm cursed and will go to my grave an inexperienced virgin haunted by the ghosts of all the penises I've never known?

With my anxiety reaching the tipping point that will send me running home to spend the night watching Hugh Jackman in *Les Mis* with Stephen King, my senile cat, even if he chews a button off my blouse like he did the other night—the cat, not the actor—I whip out my phone and place an emergency call.

Chloe, my best friend and the marketing guru who has helped make Love Cycle Creations successful beyond my wildest dreams, answers on the second ring. "Have you run home to hide yet?" she asks, proving I am a predictably predictable coward.

"No," I whisper, gliding to the edge of the balcony to stare down at the traffic zipping by below. "But I'm considering jumping off this roof and putting myself out of my misery. My date's not here."

I didn't tell Chloe that my mystery date is Graham— I'm not ready to cough up that gossip morsel—but I had to tell someone I was leaving the house to see a male of the species for the first time in nearly six months. "Why isn't he here?"

"Um, so many reasons—stalled subway car, shitty Uber driver, construction blocking a major artery to the Lower West Side? Need I go on?"

"He has a driver and a town car," I mumble, arranging myself behind a potted tree with a view of the elevator.

"Ooh la la. A fancy man, eh? You didn't tell me he was fancy," she says, barreling on before I can reply. "But still. His town car doesn't have wings, does it? He could be stuck in traffic." Chloe pauses and mumbles something under her breath along with my name, making me think she's not alone on the other end of the line.

Of course she's not. Chloe is sexy, funny, fabulous, and completely comfortable in her own skin. She loves men and they love her, and she's rarely without a man of the moment, even if she does tend to shy away from long-term relationships.

"I'm sorry," I say, feeling terrible for being the needy boss-friend who interrupts a Monday-night booty call. "Am I interrupting your evening? I can go. This isn't a big deal."

"Of course it's a big deal, and no, you're not interrupting," Chloe says. "So quit being crazy and repeat after me: I'm CJ Murphy. I am a sweet, generous person who loves animals and small children and would do anything for a friend. I also own my own company, am smoking hot, and any dude is lucky to be going on a date with me."

Lucky to be going on a date with me.

Lucky to be going on a date with me . . .

But this isn't really a date—it's a sex lesson—but I can't tell Chloe that. I'm not ready to confess that to anyone. Maybe not even myself.

I'm so much more scared than I thought I would be.

Dear God, this is really happening. Graham will be here any minute—he runs late, but he always shows—and my life is going to be changed FOREVER.

"You know what, Chloe? I think I need a drink." Tucking my purse under my arm, I make a beeline for the bar. "I'll talk to you tomorrow, okay?"

"Or call me later," Chloe says. "I want to hear how it goes! Good luck."

"Thanks." I end the call and slip onto an empty stool beneath an antique replica of a World War II fighter plane. In a heartbeat, the bartender spots me and heads my way, clearly sensing my sudden and powerful need for liquid courage.

But before I can open my mouth to order, he says, "You're CJ, right?"

I straighten, surprised. "Um, yeah. Yes."

He fetches a dirty vodka martini with extra olives, my favorite drink, from beneath the bar and slides it across the smoothly polished surface. "Your friend ordered this for you about ten minutes ago. Glad you showed. I hate to waste good vodka." He departs with a wink, leaving me even more unsettled.

There, underneath the elegant stem of the martini glass, is a folded note, my name on it in Graham's handwriting.

Drinks and winks and mysterious notes, oh my . . .

My face flushes as I reach for it. *He's going to tell me he made a mistake. He's going to tell me to go home, change into my snowman-covered flannel pajamas, and embrace my life as a person who is always on the outside looking in.*

The cool spring breeze on my exposed arms suddenly feels like ice, summoning goose bumps from my skin. With shaking hands, I unfold the note and read: *Go to the restroom.*

I wrinkle my nose and murmur, "I already peed before I came up, thank you." Who knew meeting a man who knew you so well could be so . . . completely unromantic?

But then, this isn't about romance. This is a business arrangement with pleasurable benefits, and I would be a fool to forget it. The part of me that's still a young girl with a crush on her older brother's best friend has to stay out of sight and out of mind. There's no room for her around here, only for grown-up CJ and her practical and grounded expectations.

I glance around the patio, but there's still no sign of Graham, and I confess I feel silly texting him to say I don't have to pee. Seriously, this isn't a doctor's visit where you need to whiz in a cup.

I take a small sip of my drink, then a larger one, my foot bobbing as I await the arrival of the man of the hour. The man of the week, who might very well be planting his flag in my moondust before the evening is through.

Cursing under my breath, I down the entire cocktail in one long gulp. Hell, I need it. And—bonus points—I think maybe I can pee now. If I try really hard.

Licking the sea-salty goodness from my lips, I slide off my stool and amble down the hallway toward the restrooms, already feeling looser in my limbs, my equilibrium slightly off in the three-inch peep-toe heels Chloe insisted were the only choice for a "first date."

More like first bang . . .

I take a deep breath. Then another. "That's right, cool, easy, and breathing. Always breathing," I whisper as I squint at the doors on the left, looking for the ladies' room sign. "You can do this."

I pause in front of a door marked *private*. Before my stress-and-martini-affected brain can sort out what's so hush-hush about this room, the door opens and a familiar hand clamps around my upper arm, pulling me into a darkened room, a private lounge it seems.

I blink, my pulse spiking as my eyes adjust to the dimness, and Graham chastises me in a deep voice. "Don't *ever* drink a cocktail that you haven't personally watched the bartender pour."

"Then don't order me drinks to leave with your notes." I'm impressed with how sassy I sound, despite the hammering of my heart. "And were you spying on me? That's not creepy at all."

"Creepy?" He shakes his head in the near darkness as he draws me closer, until the spicy, addictive smell of him swirls through my head, making me even dizzier than I was before. "Miss Murphy, are you trying to hurt my feelings?"

"Never," I whisper, adrenaline making my chest feel as if it's filled with a swarm of butterflies on a sugar rush. "I'm going to be very respectful of your feelings. And very appreciative of your time and attention."

"That's sweet," he murmurs. "But before you start thanking me, let me give you something to be grateful for, beautiful."

My lips part to tell him I'm already grateful, but before I can speak, his mouth finds mine, needy, urgent, hungry.

This isn't a soft and tender first kiss.

It's a downright claiming.

His big hands cup my cheeks, and as he holds my face, he devours my lips. My knees go weak. Tingles spread everywhere. My insides hum. *Holy hell.* This is kissing. This is kissing like I've never been kissed before.

I feel owned, and I relish it as his tongue explores me, his teeth nipping, his faint stubble rubbing against me. Everything, all of it, sets off a swirl of sensations inside me, making those sugar-rush butterflies spin like they're caught up in a hurricane.

I've spent so many nights dreaming about the taste and feel of him—from the days when I imagined him kissing me at homecoming, to sometime last week when I woke up from a dirty dream starring Graham in a pair of running shorts and nothing else. But no fantasy could ever have prepared me for this. He tastes exactly like I thought he would, like mint and salt and that clove-and-brown-sugar aftershave he wears.

And, oh, how I want to be thinking deep, meaningful thoughts. Or at least taking copious mental notes about how un-freaking-believable this feels, but all I can think is *Holy crap, Graham Campbell is kissing me.* He's *kissing* me, and it's the best thing that has ever happened to my mouth, bar none. Forget gourmet cupcakes and that chocolate bar from Paris. They've got nothing on this man's drop-dead sexy lips.

You're going to be hooked in one go, like a drug addict . . .

The thought flitters through my mind, funny and scary at the same time, before I lose the ability to process any thoughts or feelings aside from the intense sensation of heat—sizzling, burning, exploding like a thousand fireworks inside me.

Graham wraps his arms around my waist and tangles his fingers in my hair, holding my mouth prisoner, though there's no need. I have absolutely no urge to escape.

No, I want to be right here. Right now. With Graham kissing me as if he's never wanted anything as much in his life. His tongue, lips, teeth, and powerful chest are all pressed to mine, assuring me of his commitment to lesson one.

Oh, lesson one, you're already so much better than I could have hoped . . .

"Yes," I murmur as his lips drift down my jawline and tug aside the fabric of my blouse, baring my collarbone.

"Yes?" he echoes. "So far, so good?"

"So, so good," I assure him, my fingers driving into his thick hair as he drags his teeth across the skin at the base of my neck.

"Good. Because that's what tonight is about. Making you feel good. You shouldn't worry about pleasing any man until he's proven he can please you."

My heart beats faster, the sentiment thrilling me. Or maybe it's just that I'm already falling under this wild spell of sensation, this kiss that feels like a prelude to so much more. To everything I've never experienced but so desperately want.

Deftly, with an ease that makes this crazy thing we're doing seem wholly sane, he cups my breast, his thumb rubbing the outline of my nipple. His touch sends sparks racing through me, and my entire body screams with arousal as he tilts my head back, leaving me to stare helplessly up at the ceiling as his tongue laves my neck.

"First lesson," he rasps against my skin. "The public quickie. Tell me you're ready."

Public? Is this public?

Dim red light casts shadows on lush burgundy walls. The notes of faraway jazz music skitter through the air in this dark little room, but it feels like we're alone. Not that it really matters—right now, I would say yes to anything Graham wanted to do to me. Anything, anywhere, as long as he doesn't stop making me feel like I'm shot through with starlight.

My lips part to tell him so, but I can't seem to make my vocal cords cooperate. I can't remember ever feeling this overwhelmed by pure, electric sensation.

"Tell me," Graham urges, teasing my nipple harder through the fabric of my blouse.

"Yes!" I gasp, as his other hand skims the hem of my skirt, roughly edging it up over my thighs as my brain begins chanting *oh my God, oh my God* over and over.

"Perfect." His voice is calm and controlled, as if he isn't the least bit affected by the dark magic he's working on my body. "Now turn around for me, Butterfly."

I do as I'm told, spinning to find myself staring at my own reflection, but I don't look like myself. I look wild, hungry, and . . . sexy as hell.

"That's right. Look at how hot you are," Graham says, suddenly so close his chest presses against my back as his hands slide up the sides of my skirt, baring my thighs and then that scrap of black lace he insisted I wear. That delicate, beautiful fabric that is the only thing covering where I'm already so wet, so desperate to be touched. "You're a goddamned sex goddess."

He's right. I am, I realize as he lifts my skirt higher, smoothing his hand over my bottom as my eyes go dark with hunger.

I look like I've been possessed by the spirit of some ancient fertility goddess, a creature with no shame, only hunger, desire, and bottomless, fathomless passion.

I know it won't last, and that cautious, careful CJ will be back sooner or later, but I mean to make the most of every second, every kiss, every husky groan as Graham glides his finger beneath the lace on one side of my sexy new panties.

CHAPTER 8

GRAHAM

I've been hard as steel since the moment I put this lesson plan into motion. Now, I'm on the verge of exploding.

Holy fuck, but she's hot. Unbearably hot.

CJ, sweet, sexy CJ, is all grown up and bringing me to my knees.

That's exactly where I want to be with her, soon. I can't wait to be on my knees with my tongue between her legs, tasting her, feeling her tremble as I make her even hotter, wetter.

Why did I waste precious time stressing out about being her teacher? It's so clear now that the answer should have always been yes. Hell to the motherfucking yes.

My hands glide up her hips as I tease my fingers beneath the fabric of her barely-there lace panties, which look every bit as delicious on her as I knew they would.

"Your ass was made for fine lingerie," I murmur into

her hair. "I'm going to send you these in every single color."

"If you insist," she says, her breath catching as I draw the panties down.

"You were made for something this gorgeous." I hold her gaze in the mirror as I bare her round, firm, heart-stopping ass and the thatch of dark hair between her legs.

Fuck me, but she's perfect.

I drop to my knees, unable to resist pressing a kiss to her bare ass, kissing her once, twice, before I rake my teeth over her tender flesh.

She cries out in response, her surprised sound transforming to an exquisite moan as I drag her soaked panties all the way down to the floor and urge her to step forward, one sexy heel at a time. As soon as they're free, I fist my fingers in the fabric—the crotch is so damn wet, *Jesus*—before tossing it aside.

She's every bit as turned on as I am, hands now braced on the mirror to steady herself, and it's probably going to kill me. I'm going to be dead by the time we're done, but hell, what a way to go.

I stand, draw her back to my front, and run a finger along the seam of her pussy. She melts against my body as I glide back and forth through her slick, swollen flesh. She's so ready, so eager, and the sweet, sexy scent of her is driving me insane. I explore her gently, pulsing and teasing, her gasps and moans like music in my ears. She arches her spine, trembling as I reach her throbbing clit. I slide my fingers across it, and she gasps, the sound of her sheer, unadulterated pleasure making my dick impossibly harder.

She tosses her head back, her fingers clawing at the glass in front of her as I trace circles across that swollen bundle of nerves.

"Oh, Graham," she murmurs, her voice a shot of desire into my veins. "It's so good. I had no idea it could be so good."

"And it's only going to get better," I promise as I slowly, gently, press a finger inside her, making her gasp. Jesus Christ, she's tight, incredibly tight.

Pinning her closer against my chest, I nibble on her earlobe as I go deeper, my thumb rubbing her clit at the same time. She cries out again—whether from the bite or the finger fucking, I don't know, but I'm hoping it's both, it's everything, it's all the heat and fire we're creating in this dark, secret room.

"I can't wait to hear you come," I say, my cock so hard she can surely feel it pressing against the curve of her sweet ass. "Are you going to come for me, Butterfly?"

She nods and whimpers softly. "God, I think so. I think I'm close . . ."

My rhythm falters for a moment as a tragic suspicion sweeps through me. I know she's never had sex, but surely . . .

"Have you ever come, baby?" I ask gently.

"N-not with someone else around." Her eyes slide closed as embarrassment tightens her features.

I freeze for a nanosecond, processing this new info. Lesson one is apparently going to be even more of a leap than I'd assumed.

But I'm going to make damn sure that leap is more than worth it. Silently, I thank the stupid bastards who didn't break their tongues making her come, because I get to be the first to coax a delicious, intoxicating orgasm from her.

And I won't fail.

"That's about to change," I rasp out.

Her lips press together, but her eyes stay closed. "It's my fault. I get nervous and I can't—" Her words break off with a soft cry as I rub her clit in another firm circle and then another. "I-I can't . . ."

"Shh, baby. You can," I promise. "And you will."

Or I will die trying, I add silently, completely ready to give my life if that's what it takes to bring my beautiful, sexy CJ to the other side of the cliff. I will deliver her first orgasm right here, right now, or I don't deserve to walk out the door still pretending to be a man.

CHAPTER 9

CJ

I open my eyes in time to see my cheeks flush scarlet in the mirror and Graham watching me over my shoulder. His big, strong hands and wickedly talented fingers continue to work between my legs, building the swell of pleasure that threatens to pull me under any second.

I want to be pulled. I want to fall. Pleasure crawls up my legs, curls tight in my belly. I'm on the edge, so close I can taste it. I've brought myself here countless times. I've flown off the edge to so many fantasies. I know how it feels, the delicious pressure, the intense waves. But what will it be like when I don't have to work for every ounce of it solo?

My lashes flutter, but Graham shakes his head, holding my gaze.

"Keep those eyes open, gorgeous. Let me see you get hotter for me."

With my arms trembling, I press my fingers flat against the glass as he palms a breast, squeezing and kneading as his other hand rocks between my legs. I climb higher, higher, until the air is so thick with desire I can barely breathe.

I'm shaking. I'm shaking everywhere, panting and moaning, and I can barely take all these wild sensations chasing through me.

"I love turning you on," he says, his breath hot in my ear. "You're the sweetest, sexiest thing I've ever felt, and the smell of you makes me crazy."

I gasp as the steel rod of his erection presses more firmly into the small of my back. I'm too drunk on everything to speak. Pleasure, anticipation, fear, desire . . . all surging, pulsing, building. This feeling is beyond anything I expected, anything I could have imagined before I knew what it felt like to be in Graham's arms.

His mouth is on my neck, devouring my skin, his tongue sending waves of electricity coursing through my body as he picks up speed with his hand. The driving rhythm makes every nerve vibrate with a terrible, beautiful longing.

In all the times I've given myself pleasure, I've never felt anything like this. I'm crazy, wild, lost, but so close to being found.

So close, so close . . .

God, yes . . .

"Graham!" I buck against him, meeting his thrusts. Now he has two fingers inside me, stretching me, moving harder and faster, his thumb racing over my clit as I ride his hand. And suddenly, there it is, that deep, desperate pull between my legs, in my stomach, rising higher, tighter until it bursts.

I come so hard my vision blurs, and I have to bite my

tongue to stop from screaming. Shudders rack my body, and pleasure washes over my skin, lapping sweet and vicious inside my bones until I know I will never be the same.

I press my bare lower body against Graham and my cheek against the cold mirror, ready for him to pull away, but he clearly has no intention of stopping. His fingers continue their nimble work, thrusting and rubbing. Before I've fully recovered from the first time —my first non-solo flight *ever*—I've re-boarded the roller coaster, swooping down and then up, up—

This time, I nearly stop breathing.

This time, I don't just leave earth. I leave my body, soaring skyward as bliss pulses through me, changing me, transforming me. Teaching me things I've never known before. Dark, delicious secrets that can only be communicated when two people are skin to skin.

As I drift down through puffy, orgasm-colored clouds, Graham withdraws his hand from between my legs and gently but firmly guides my mouth to his. He kisses me deep, hard, but-oh-so sweet, sending heat spreading through my chest.

"You're incredible," he murmurs against my lips.

Am I? Really? I haven't done anything for him.

At least, not yet . . .

Oh, but I want to. I want it almost as badly as I wanted the release he coaxed out of me like the master of pleasure he is.

I really did pick the best teacher in the entire history of the world.

I reach back, running my hand up the length of his hardness through his pants. But before I can do more than touch—before I can even come to terms with just how *large* he is down there—he bats my hand away.

"Not now," he says, his voice tight, almost irritated.

I straighten my spine, embarrassed. "But I want . . . You're supposed to, I mean . . . I mean, *I'm* supposed to . . ." I stop, my face burning as I ease my skirt over my hips.

Graham, however? He just leans back against the wall, smoothing his shirt calmly as he shrugs. "Don't worry about 'supposed to' right now, okay? I'm the teacher, remember?"

I swallow. "I-I know. And that was wonderful." *Life-altering is more like it. I still can't feel my feet.* "But I want to learn how to drive men wild."

And how to drive you *wild in particular . . .*

"Mission accomplished, gorgeous. But this is as far as we go tonight."

Before I can respond, he leans down, kissing me like I'm the heroine of a classic movie. He kisses me like they used to kiss when films were black and white and passion had to fill in for all the other colors. He kisses me like I've always dreamed of being kissed—like I'm the one, the girl, the long-lost lover-friend my man has been looking for—before whispering, "Until next time, Butterfly," and slipping out the door.

"Graham?" I squeak, but he doesn't come back. He's gone.

Lesson one is over.

Still shell-shocked, I blink faster, looking around our small, private lounge, my hand flying to cover my mouth when I spot the enormous floor-to-ceiling window on the far wall. The one with a view high above the streets of Manhattan and the lights blazing in the windows of the building on the other side of the street. Which means—

Someone could have seen.

Well, duh, that's the point of a public quickie.

I drag in a deep breath, wondering what the heck I've gotten myself into. Lesson one was insanely good, yes. Better than I'd even hoped. Almost *too* good.

So good it felt . . . dangerous somehow.

No matter how much I trust Graham, I don't know if I trust myself.

Do I have what it takes to fly that high, that close, without sustaining life-shattering injuries in the process? Sure, I know Graham would never hurt my body, but what about my heart? That squishy, love-hungry organ that has always been way too sweet on Graham Campbell for its own good?

As long as I keep my head up, I've got this. There's no reason my heart needs to overextend itself. This is a seven-days-to-seduction deal, and like any good business arrangement, you simply see it through, brush your hands, and move on when you're done.

"Woman up," I say to myself. "You're a big girl. You can do this. You have to do this, and you will be just fine."

Smart or not, I *must* see this through. After what I just experienced, I'm more certain than ever that I have Grand-Canyon-size gaps in my erotic knowledge, gaps that only Graham can help me fill. Too bad I have plans tomorrow night, but I'm confident he'll give me extra credit work the next time I see him.

After taking a few more deep breaths and smoothing

the worst of the wrinkles from my skirt, I find my panties on the floor. Stuffing them in my purse, I totter out the door and make my way unsteadily through the bar. It's grown more crowded—a good thing, since no one seems to notice the disheveled, sex-rumpled girl making her way to the elevators. In the lobby, I charge past the line of people waiting for a taxi.

Time to walk this off, girlfriend.

My head is still swimming. My feet are giant gummy bears that wobble unsteadily beneath me as I plod the ten blocks to my apartment building. Sounds are louder. Lights are brighter. The world has shifted. I've walked home at night a million times, but suddenly, everything is different, sparkling, dusted in magic.

I'm floating up the two stories to my apartment's front door when my phone hums in my purse.

GRAHAM: Home safe?

I SMILE, heat rushing to my face again as I remember his hands on me, erasing the memory of all hands that had been there before.

Before I can reply that yes, I'm home, another text hums through.

GRAHAM: Sending you something to help you get to sleep, though I hope you realize only crazy people read horror novels before bed. Assuming you haven't bought this one yet, since it just released yesterday.

I GRIN as I open my e-reader app to see the newest hide-under-the-covers read by my favorite mistress of horror. I tap out a thank you as I close my apartment door behind me.

CJ: Thank you so much! I can't wait to read it. You're a genius.

GRAHAM: Sleep well, sweetheart, and don't stay up too late. You need to rest up for lesson two. I know you're busy tomorrow, so I'll see you on Wednesday. Be ready.
Lesson two . . .
Oh my God, lesson two.
I shiver, my thumbs quivering as I reply.

CJ: Will do. Thank you and . . . good night.

GRAHAM: Good night . . .

LESSON TWO, ready or not, here I come . . .

CHAPTER 10

GRAHAM

*N*ever-ending first-Tuesday-of-the-month status meetings are par for the course at Adored. But since efficiency is my watchword, we can usually make it through them in less than an hour.

That's due in part to Sean's legacy.

He was a master at getting things done fast, smoothly, and right-the-first-time. I learned a lot from him. If I run into a thorny situation at work, I'll often ask myself what he would have done.

The trouble is, as I wonder briefly how to quell the shareholders' urge to slap up a "for sale" sign prematurely, I fight like hell to *not* think of him.

Because of what I did to his sister last night.

I glance at the photo on the wall of the conference room, one of Sean and me at a hockey game shortly after Adored went public. We were having the time of our lives, rooting for our team and high on the success of our new public venture. Now, though? I see him up in heaven, banging a fist on the cloudy floor, wanting to know why the fuck I thought it was okay to show his baby sister how to come so hard she saw stars.

"And that's what we have going on in distribution," Debra says, the bespectacled head of that department finishing her status report.

"Great. Fantastic." I turn to goateed Taylor, who's up next with a download on production.

As he talks about factory capacity, my mind drifts dangerously again to CJ, her hot body clenching on me when she came. She was so tight, and it felt fucking amazing, but the best part was how abandoned and shameless she was, rocking against me, chasing her own pleasure.

She shook me to my core.

How could she do that? Be so innocent and yet mind-blowingly sexy at the same time? That's what's driving me crazy. She's a beguiling mix of contradictions—a wildly sensual woman and yet a virgin.

I want her again. Right here. Right now. Want to push up her skirt and slide into her.

But. She. Is. My. Partner's. Sister.

Oh yeah, and I'm in a meeting.

I do my best to refocus, but Taylor already gave me a heads-up on this yesterday, and I have more pressing things on my mind. I like to take my time with a woman, explore her body, drive her wild with pleasure, but I'm not really known for going gentle and easy. That's not my MO. And I've never been with a virgin, not even when I was one. Hell, I lost my virginity to a woman who was way more experienced. She was four years older and knew exactly what she wanted, and I was a lucky son-of-a-bitch that she was willing to deal with my teenage self.

But I'm a guy. I didn't need coaxing along the road to sexual self-realization.

Now, with CJ, I'm . . . concerned.

What if I scare her or, God forbid, hurt her without meaning to? I could never forgive myself.

What if I lose control and take her hard, fucking her up against a wall because I just can't hold back. Can't take another second of being so close but not close enough?

That's why I left so abruptly last night. Staying there, breathing her in with her body so warm and smelling like sex, would have killed my resolve. I had to get the hell out of her sensuality zone and cool off.

Though cool isn't the best adjective to describe the scenes that played out in my head when I returned home, unzipped my pants, and came in my hand mere minutes after the door shut behind me.

But cool, calm, and collected is how I'll have to be for lesson two. Sucks that I have to wait another night to get my hands on her since she has theater tickets tonight. Fucking *Hamilton*. But I'm sure I'm not the first guy to play second banana to that musical.

I drag my fingers through my hair before dropping my hand to the armrests of the leather chair Sean once occupied. I move them to my lap as if I've been burned by the ghost who's haunting me, whispering in my ear, *If you hurt her, I will break your fucking back.*

And he would. He absolutely would.

But I don't want to hurt her. I only want to bring her pleasure.

"Graham?"

I swivel around. My COO Christopher stares at me from across the table, expecting a response. And I've no idea what item on the agenda he's referring to, or when the hell we moved from Taylor to Christopher.

Plus, I'm sporting an incredibly inconvenient erection.

Shit. Time to call upon the old standby. I imagine them all naked. As horrifying an image as that is—it will require bleach to wipe it away—it does the trick.

I tap my fingers on the conference table. "Yeah, I was thinking about that one," I bluff. I can't let on that my mind wandered. Not with the board vote next week. Besides, I'm supposed to be on a sex-batical, not an intensive immersion course. I need to act like my brain isn't hanging out on naughty shores all day long.

"Yes?" Christopher leans forward.

I heave a deep sigh. The kind that says a thoughtful answer is coming.

"And I wonder if we're ready for that yet?" I say, figuring this is like the SAT. If you don't know the answer, you take a guess. That seems like a reasonable response to any question that might have arisen.

Christopher furrows his brow. "We're not ready to move up the release of the new corsets? We just secured space for them in our lineup."

Oops.

Wrong guess.

But am I CEO or am I CEO?

I lean back in my chair, let a slow smile spread, and point at him. "Gotcha." I slap the table. "Of course we're ready. We're ready to launch that rocket into the holiday stratosphere. Santa's going to have a bag full of naughty this Christmas."

I'm rewarded with cheers and laughter.

I stand, give a quick wave, and say, "I have an important call to make. Good work, good focus, and great hustle."

That earns me some smiles for keeping the meeting on time.

Inside my office, I close the door and will my mind to concentrate on the mountain of work that awaits me. With iron focus and sheer determination, I power my way through the afternoon.

In the early evening, I take off, saying goodbye to Brian. "Don't work too late."

He shuts his laptop. "I'm on my way out now. I need to head home to Missy and bring her some pepper steak. She's been craving that like mad the last few weeks."

"How far along is she now?"

"Thirty-seven weeks."

I clap him on the back. "Excellent. And is everything going well?"

"Perfectly. Knock on wood."

"Send her my best, and on the way home, why don't you pick up some takeout from the Hunan Garden around the corner? Put it on my personal account."

A grin spreads across his face. "I really appreciate that."

"My pleasure."

A productive day at work, a gesture of goodwill toward a colleague and his lady, and a hard workout in my future—it's all good. But I can't help wishing CJ were going to be with me tonight.

I'd really like to take her to night school. Right now.

* * *

AFTER A MUSCLE-BURNING and heart-pounding five-mile run, followed by an intense session of weights, I've exhausted my body and distracted my mind.

At home, I pour myself a Scotch and settle in to catch up on one of my favorite flicks of all time, *Office Space*. At this point, I can recite it as I watch, including the bit where the douche boss in his blue shirt and white cuffs monotones the line that makes every employee cringe. "Yeah, I'm going to need you to come in on Saturday."

But rather than laughing at a too-true bit, I'm back where I started the day.

With CJ.

Bending her over my desk.

Working overtime on her body. Making her come on a Saturday. A Sunday. Hell, *every* day.

Damn, I'm an easy bastard, managing to get hard watching a dark comedy.

I glance down at the tent in my shorts. *Thanks, CJ, for yet another erection courtesy of you.* Tomorrow—and lesson two—can't come soon enough.

I flick off the TV, since there's no way I'm going to take care of this while Bill Lumbergh, the douche boss from the flick, is on the screen.

But my office is where I'd like to see CJ.

Perched on the edge of my desk. Knees up, heels on,

panties off. I flash back to the softness of her skin, damp with sweat, and the incredible way she'd smelled, like innocence meets desire.

My dick stretches against my boxer briefs, demanding attention. Persistent bastard. Didn't I fucking deal with him this morning in the shower already?

But I heed the call.

I push down my briefs and draw out my cock, like an iron spike already. No surprise, I suppose. I've been operating at attention nearly all day. I close my hand over my shaft, my skin hot to the touch. I close my eyes, remembering the sexy sounds CJ made as she neared the edge, the sweet taste of her skin. My blood rushes hot and fast as I stroke from base to tip, my thoughts lingering on the way her eyes widened when she'd touched my dick, the sheer excitement in her gaze, like a wild thrill was rushing through her. Like she wanted to touch my dick as much as I wanted her to.

I grip harder, jerk faster, picturing spreading her open on my desk.

My dick aches for release, like it has all day, and finally, finally, I'm going to get there. I'm dying to taste her, to bury my face in her pussy. A bolt of pleasure shoots down my spine as I imagine driving my tongue inside her, sucking on her clit, making her come so hard I can feel her all over my mouth, my face. Then flipping her over, and fucking her hard on the edge of my desk. Bent over at the waist, her skirt hiked up. Begging for more. Begging for me to fuck her harder, faster.

Please, she'd cry, in the most desperate voice I've ever heard. *Please don't stop, Graham.*

As my tempo speeds up, I hear her voice in my head, begging me to come inside her, and that's all it takes. An orgasm barrels down my spine, and I come hard, my hips shooting up.

Aftershocks radiate through me, my body still shuddering with the image of that intoxicating woman.

Heading to the bathroom, I wash my hands and clean up.

I shouldn't want this. I shouldn't want her this much. But even though I know better than to let my libido get away from me, I can hardly wait for tomorrow.

And I decide part of being her teacher is letting her know that.

I settle back on my couch, take a hearty drink of my Scotch, and grab my phone.

GRAHAM: Hope the show was great tonight. Just so you know, I can't stop thinking about how sexy you are.

CJ: The show was PHENOMENAL, and you were pretty damn sexy yourself. (How's that for a flirty compliment, teacher?)

I LAUGH and tap out a reply.

GRAHAM: I'm giving you an A+ in everything.

CJ: Confession: I always did enjoy earning high marks in school.

GRAHAM: I'm not surprised that you were an excellent student. You take direction exceedingly well.

CJ: And that extends to the lovely white box you sent me tonight. I'm not quite sure how to put it on with all these straps, but I'll figure it out. Hopefully without accidentally tying myself up in the process.

I SMILE AT THE IMAGE.

GRAHAM: If there's any tying up to be done, I'll be doing it.

CJ: I can't say I would mind that being on the lesson plan . . .

AND IT'S OFFICIALLY time to switch from texting to calling.

She answers on the first ring. "Hey, you."

"Hey to you, too," I say, a stupid grin forming on my face just from hearing her voice. "How was your evening?"

"It was great. My Macy's rep really enjoyed the show, and we talked business during intermission. They're going to be stocking my entire line of recycled typewriter-key jewelry in the fall. And I think I've almost talked her into taking a few of my signature collection pieces for the Christmas displays. I should know next week since they plan those so far in advance. Which reminds me, I was thinking about the Adored board meeting. Is there anything I should prepare? I know I said I'd tap-dance on the table, but honestly, that probably won't help your cause seeing as I can't, you know, *actually* tap-dance."

"Glad you asked. I've been giving it some thought, and two key points come to mind. I'd love you to share a little bit about the offer you had a year ago, when you chose not to sell, and how that decision was the right one. And I think just a general statement about my commitment to the company your brother and I built together would be great. With the way companies swap hands these days, and how quickly CEOs change their minds, these guys just need reassurance that I'm in it for the long haul, so *they* stay in it for the long haul." Maybe it wouldn't be such a bad idea to show CJ the corsets, especially given how critical the marketing is to the next growth phase for the company. "Although, there is this other thing. Are you online?"

She scoffs. "Am I online? When is anyone in our modern world not online or able to get online in, say, ten seconds?"

"When my hand is in your panties. That's when you can't get online."

Silence greets me, and for a brief second, I fear I've overstepped the mark.

I'm finally rewarded with her laughter, and I can

picture her perfectly—her smile, her twinkling brown eyes, her pretty lips curving up as she chuckles.

"Well, yes, that would indeed be an obstacle, Graham." She clears her throat. "And to answer your question, yes, I have my laptop open."

"Let me show you what we're working on. Check out slides ten to twelve."

I send her my file, and when she clicks it open, I hear her appreciative gasp.

"These are so pretty." Her admiring tone sets off pride fireworks in my chest. It's nice to know someone with taste as exquisite as CJ's likes my work. "I love the light-blue one, and the beadwork on the pink is stunning."

"Would you ever wear one?"

She pauses. "Hmm." She seems to be considering my question. "Well, yes, but probably not for the reasons you think."

Her response intrigues me. I sit up straighter. "What are the reasons I think?"

"Your tagline. *Have your cake and wear it, too . . .* That makes it seem like this piece is all about the function of holding in my cake belly, or maybe making me look like a piece of cake to someone else. But personally, I'm thinking more about how wearing one would make me feel. The pink one, for example, you could totally wear that for a night out with jeans and a shawl. I can imagine how sexy and feminine that would make me feel. How confident, you know?"

I nod, the cogs in my brain turning. "Brian and I were brainstorming how to make the marketing work better. I'll have to talk that over with him. It's an angle we missed."

She laughs gently. "Probably because you've never worn one. Or is there something you want to share with me, Graham? Don't be embarrassed. I'm an accepting person, and it takes all kinds to make the world turn."

I crack up, as I scrub a hand over my jaw. "I assure you that my fascination with women's underthings comes from my desire to see a beautiful woman in them, and then out of them. Not from any secret cross-dressing tendencies."

"Good." She sighs softly. "I'm looking forward to tomorrow."

"Me, too."

"And tonight I have this scary clown to keep me company until bedtime. Thank you so much for the thoughtful gift."

I groan. "That's what the book I bought you is about? If I'd known, I would never have gifted it," I tease. "I am morally opposed to the perpetuation of scary clown stories. How can horror fans seriously enjoy them? They're a messed-up kind of terrifying."

"They are. And that's exactly why we like them," she says with a laugh.

"Twisted," I breathe. "Tell me more. What other messed-up things do you enjoy being scared by, Miss Murphy?"

I settle into my couch and listen to her tell me why she loves horror novels—they make her feel wildly, electrically alive.

"And is Mr. King one of your favorites, like he was for Sean?" I ask.

"He is indeed. Though, when Sean adopted Stevie from the shelter, I suggested Tiger Lily as a name, for my favorite flower. And because Steve has freckles on his nose like the flower petals. But, being all macho man, Sean stuck with Stephen King."

I smile at the image she paints of my best friend. "I can picture that conversation clearly."

"He made the right choice, though. I swear this cat is addicted to books, too. He runs over to sit on me as soon as I crack one open."

"It's good of you to take care of him." I remember driving CJ to pick up Stephen King at Sean's place the day he was killed. *He'd want me to take care of Steve, to make sure he doesn't go back to a shelter*, she'd said amid tears that seemed to flow endlessly.

She sighs, a little wistful, a little sad. "It's easy, really. And Sean loved this cat. The least I can do is look out for him like he would have," she says, before adding in a lighter tone, "but my next pet is going to be a hedgehog. I'm obsessed with their cuteness."

"Then you're going to have to move out of the boroughs, baby. Hedgehogs are illegal in the city."

"No!" she gasps. "You're kidding."

"I'm not. My friend Luna was going to get one for her wife, but the rescue group said they can't adopt them to city-dwellers."

We talk some more, and I find myself enjoying this phone call more than I ever expected to when I picked up the phone . . .

. . . an hour ago.

We just passed an hour, chatting about everything

and nothing, and this very well might be my favorite hour so far today.

"Thanks for your thoughts on the new line," I say as we sign off, both agreeing it's time to head for bed so we can get up and conquer the world tomorrow. "They were helpful. I'm going to mull them over with Brian tomorrow."

"My pleasure," she murmurs in a husky, sleepy voice that makes me wish I were there to tuck her in—and to get a jump start on the pleasure I have planned for lesson two.

"Sleep tight, sexy," I say. "I'll be dreaming about all the things I'm going to do to your body."

Her breath rushes out. "Me, too. Not even scary clowns will be able to keep those dreams away."

"Good." I hang up with a grin and another hard-on. Because that's what this woman does to me. It's almost embarrassing, but that's not going to stop me from bringing my thoughts of CJ into bed with me tonight and taking things . . . *ahem* . . . in hand one more time.

Three times in one day—I haven't been this determined with my self-love since I was a teenager.

I'm not sure what my sexy little virgin is doing to my libido, but I don't want it to stop. Not any time soon.

But as I glance at my phone one last time before bed, the date stares at me. We didn't even have a lesson tonight, and already our seven days of seduction is now down to five.

CHAPTER 11

CJ

There's something wrong, but I can't quite put my finger on it.

"You're sure this is the exact same design as the mock-up you sent over yesterday?" I tilt my head to one side, squinting at the printout of the ad Chloe is going to run on social media as soon as I give it the thumbs-up.

Usually, I can spot the puzzle piece that doesn't fit in sixty seconds or less, but my instincts are dull today. I would blame chatting late with Graham, but it wasn't the chat that was the problem. It's the hours I lay awake afterward replaying every kiss, every touch, every word he spoke to me at Patio West, and imagining all the things we might get up to together tonight.

Sexy things. Erotic things. Exciting, exhilarating, life-changingly amazing things that had me up until way past midnight giving Sparky the Wonder Vibrator a workout he hasn't seen in months.

All I want to do is replay Graham and CJ's Greatest Hits over and over until my brain turns to mush—but focus *must* be achieved.

I have three thousand up-cycled, vintage hardcover-books-turned-adorable-purses in my warehouse in Georgia, already wrapped in tissue paper and ready to ship. I need to get them out into the world to make room for the typewriter-key earrings my production team is hard at work on for next season.

The purses *must* be advertised and sold. I must get this ad exactly right. And I *must stop thinking about sex* for at least the next five to ten minutes.

"Is her dress a different color?" I ask, shaking my head as the backs of my eyes begin to ache.

"No, the dress is the same." Chloe crosses her arms over her chest as she perches on my desk beside me. I sit on my desk more than I sit behind it. I've always been the kind of person who thinks better on her feet. "I did tweak the background filter the tiniest bit, but—"

"That's it." I snap my fingers, pointing at the sky behind the model's head. Thank God, I haven't lost it—yet. "The new shade of yellow is making her skin look sallow, and that's throwing the rest of the color scheme off just a hair."

"I thought it made the purse pop." Chloe hums beneath her breath. "But you're right. She looks like she has food poisoning. Sorry about that. Maybe my monitor needs to be recalibrated."

I wave a hand. "No worries. Let's just shift it back and take another look."

Chloe accepts the printout but doesn't move from

her perch. "Totally. I'll get right on that as soon as you serve up the gossip. And I want every detail, Murphy. I've given you almost forty-eight hours alone with your dirty little secrets. Now, it's dish time."

"Who says I have dirty secrets?" I circle back behind my desk to mark "meet with Chloe" off my list—the only thing more fun than making lists is marking things off them.

Oh, and being semi-naked with Graham with his hands all over me and his lips hot on mine. That's definitely way more fun than anything list-related.

"Um, your face." Chloe tosses her blond curls over her shoulder as she turns to pin me with one of her always-sees-through-me looks. "The goofy grin and the dreamy expression. The way you keep biting your lip to keep from smiling and then smiling anyway. And giggling. So much giggling, Murphy. It's just silly."

"I am not giggling," I scoff, fighting the urge to giggle because that's what happens when you're determined *not* to do something.

"And the sudden appearance of eye makeup," Chloe continues, ticking items off on her fingers, "and perfume, and strappy shoes, and the fact that you've worn sexy dresses to the office two days in a row."

I glance down then back up at Chloe with an arched brow. "I didn't realize a simple, black, short-sleeve dress was a sexy choice."

Chloe sighs. "Just tell me who's romancing the happy into you, CJ, so I can do my due diligence as your best friend, google his ass ten ways to next Wednesday, and make sure he's worthy of you."

Romancing me? No way. There will be no romance

between Graham and me. It's all business. Well, the business of pleasure. I snicker quietly at my own private joke.

Chloe wags a finger in the air between us. "No lies in this office. That's rule number one, and you wrote the rules."

I bite my lip, but this time fighting back a smile has nothing to do with it.

Chloe knows Graham. She's even joined us for happy hour a few times in the Village on her way back to Brooklyn on her bike. More importantly, she knows Graham's reputation as a ladies' man. She's usually not the kind to judge a guy for something like that, but Chloe also knows about my . . . unique situation.

I twist my lips to one side and then the other, possessed by the warring urges to keep my sex ed plan under wraps and to finally share with someone the monumental changes taking place in my life.

Especially a friend I know I can trust.

"Okay." I glance over her shoulder and then circle to close the door to my office. I don't mind dishing with Chloe, but the rest of the staff doesn't need the scoop on the status of my still amazingly intact virginity.

I snick the door closed and turn with a deep breath to face her. "So, first up, I want to assure you that this was my idea, I know exactly what I'm getting into, and my expectations are totally in line with what my friend is prepared to deliver."

Chloe's usually sunshiny expression transforms to a frown. "Uh-oh. I don't like the sound of this. You always say you know what you're getting into right before you do something insane, like bid three times over asking price for *Hamilton* tickets, or decide to bike to the Jersey shore, or foster a litter of abandoned baby pit bulls that pee on every pair of shoes you own."

I shake my head. "It's nothing like that. Nothing that's going to end badly, though I did discover an incredible junkyard on my way to Jersey before I pulled the hamstring, and the pit bulls were adopted by great families, and Stephen King managed not to get eaten by one. Plus, our Macy's rep loved the musical, and it totally softened her up about holiday product placement. So I'm saying all's well that ends well."

Her frown becomes a scowl.

"Fine." I lift my arms in surrender. Clearly I need to spit it out before her imagination runs wild. "I wasn't out on a first date Monday night. I was having my first lesson with Graham. He's agreed to be my sex ed teacher."

Chloe's green eyes bulge.

"And it went really well," I say, hurrying on. "And pretty soon I'm going to know everything I want to know about being a man-magnet and finally have my V card punched in the process. It's a win-win. All win. Total win."

And I just said "win" four times.

My repetition does not go unnoticed. "So, what you're saying is, you're winning?" Chloe counters slowly, taking her time with each word. "At least until you crack your head open on the bottom of the pool because you went right from the wading area to jumping off the high dive at the Olympics." Her expression grows distinctly concerned. "CJ, you know I like Graham, but he's a . . . and you're a . . ." She waves her hand up and down, gesturing to me from head to toe.

"I'm a pigeon, and he's a bald eagle?" I suggest.

Chloe snorts. "Um, I was thinking more a shark and a baby seal, but okay. Eagles eat pigeons, right?"

"Actually, they eat fish. But Graham is not going to eat me," I say, then a scandalized snort escapes my lips as I realize how that sounds. "Sorry." I wave a hand in front of my face as I swallow the burst of laughter because, of course, he's going to do just that. And soon, I hope. "I shouldn't be going there. I'm not open to talking specifics. That stays between Graham and me."

"Does it?" She arches a honey-colored brow. "Because last time I checked, Graham wasn't the kind who minded everyone knowing who he was fucking, how often, and in what kinky positions."

"That's not Graham," I say, jumping to his defense. "He doesn't kiss-and-tell. His exes are the ones who talk."

"And how many of them are there? Fifty? One hundred? Two hundred?" Chloe bites her lip. "You did have Mr. Man Whore tested before you jumped on his pony, right? I'm worried about your health, you know, not just your heart."

"Graham would never expose me to anything that would hurt me," I say firmly, not a sliver of doubt in my mind. "He's clean. He cares about me. And we are both approaching this as adults who are friends and are deeply respectful of each other." I wiggle my shoulders back and forth. "And we haven't gotten to the pony-riding yet, but soon, maybe. Maybe very soon."

Chloe nods for a long moment, her lips pursing,

then squishing into a wiggly line, then spreading into a melancholy smile.

"What?" I ask, flopping a hand her way. "What does that smile medley mean, exactly?"

"It means I believe you," Chloe says slowly. "And I hope everything goes exactly as planned." She pauses before adding in a careful tone, "And I'm here for you any time you need to vent or cry, and I promise not to say I told you so."

I cross my arms over my chest. "Just tell me I can handle this, okay?"

She smiles again, more sympathetically this time. "Like I said, I'll be here to catch you when you fall. Or *if* you fall." She shrugs. "Who knows, it could work out great. Crazier things have happened."

"That's true," I agree. "Crazier things happen all the time."

"Especially in this city. Which reminds me, Roberto asked me to make sure you wanted to shoot the apron samples on that urban farm in Brooklyn," she says with an eloquent roll of her eyes. "He seems to think aprons only belong in a kitchen."

I cluck my tongue in exaggerated disapproval. "Silly Roberto. Of course I want to shoot at the farm. And I want the models wearing nothing but swimsuits and aprons. It's going to be so sexy and fun." I nod, thinking back to my conversation with Graham last night as I add, "And I want the girls to have such a good time that everyone who sees these photos thinks about what a blast they'll have in an adorable, retro-style apron."

Chloe's expression takes on an appraising air.

"Agreed. I like your embracing of the sexy. Maybe Graham will be good for you, after all."

I cast my eyes to the ceiling with a breezy laugh, playing it cool. "Could be. Definitely a possibility."

But inside, I'm not anything close to cool. I'm hot, bothered, eager, and so excited to see Graham again that for the rest of the day, time seems to crawl at a snail's pace. A sea slug crossing the ocean floor against an incoming tide would move faster than the clock.

I'm beginning to think the day is never going to end when a text pops up from Graham at four thirty.

GRAHAM: St. Regis sleepover. You and me. Meet me in the lobby bar at six, and we can go up together. Be sure to bring your new present so I can show you how to put it on properly. And of course, how to take it off . . .

I RUN my finger over those last few words, as tingles spread through my chest. *How to take it off . . .*

My heart beats faster, and my spirits lift. Only ninety more minutes and I'll be seeing Graham again. Ninety more minutes.

It's nothing.

It's forever.

It's going to be over in four more nights.

I close my eyes, trying to push that last errant thought out of my head. Of course it's going to end. It's designed to end. It's a seven-day project, like a week-long sex-cation.

And on that note, I let my mind wander to the kind of sex-cation we might be having tonight.

As dirty, sexy images flash before my eyes, I'm pretty sure I just did that goofy lip-bite, smile-fighting, smile-anyway thing Chloe was teasing me about before.

But who cares? Ninety minutes . . .

I can't wait.

CHAPTER 12

GRAHAM

The St. Regis lobby bar is an old standby for me. With its vintage leather seats, warm wood accents, and art deco murals depicting sun-drenched vistas and a larger-than-life King Cole attended by fawning jesters, it's simultaneously opulent and grounded in reality. Even kings fall prey to fools, and golden afternoons only last so long. For me, the St. Regis encourages thoughtful celebration.

I drank a Scotch here with Sean after we signed a lease on a new office space for Adored, courtesy of our stocks selling for more than we ever dreamed and our company expanding.

I had a martini with Luna here the night before her wedding and talked about what it meant to forsake all others, and how scary that was for her, even though she couldn't imagine spending her life with anyone but Valerie.

Hell, I treated CJ to Sunday morning mimosas here on her twenty-fifth birthday not quite a year ago, back when she was just a friend I was proud to see becoming a strong, successful woman in spite of the hell she'd been through the year before.

It had seemed only natural to suggest we meet here in this luxurious, classy place where I come to celebrate. These lessons feel like something worth celebrating, and I would be telling dirty, filthy lies if I said I hadn't been looking for a good excuse to rent out the Tiffany suite.

CJ is going to look fucking stunning framed by crystal chandeliers, priceless works of art, and Tiffany-blue walls, wearing nothing but Adored's signature Madison Avenue corset, garter belt, and white silk stockings ...

A moment later, as if summoned by my oh-so appreciative thoughts, a sweet voice calls out from the entrance to the bar. I turn on my stool to see CJ bustling toward me in a sexy little black dress—I'm a sucker for a demure collar and a hemline barely long enough to cover a woman's ass—and four-inch heels that prompt erotic visions of her in those and nothing else.

"Hey there," she says, pressing a breathless kiss to my cheek and pulling away with a flustered smile. She drops her black jacket on the chair next to me. "Sorry. Am I late?"

My breath catches as I spy a glimpse of lacy corset through the peek-a-boo paisley eyelets sewn into the bodice of her dress. That tiny window is even sexier than a view straight down the front of her shirt. It hints at things concealed under her clothes, things she's going to share only with me. Like the corset I sent her yesterday, the one I chose just for her. All I can picture is how enticing it'll look against her skin.

Then, how much better it'll look on the floor of the hotel room.

"No, you're good. I'm just early," I say, fighting what feels like my fiftieth CJ-inspired erection of the day.

"*Early*," she echoes, her eyes going wide. "Is this a first for you? I mean, I know you're always on time to work, but in a social setting, isn't five minutes late your modus operandi?"

"No," I lie, then immediately fess up because lying to CJ feels wrong. "Okay, maybe, but I don't believe in keeping my students waiting. Especially my favorite students."

Her lashes sweep down and back up, and a smile that's pure sex kitten curves her lips. "I believe I'm your *only* student, Professor Campbell."

"You can be both my only and my favorite, Miss Murphy," I say, losing the battle against the thickening situation in my pants. But seriously, there's only so much a man can take.

She reaches up, her fingertips skimming over the skin exposed by my open collar. "What are you teaching me tonight? I came dressed as requested."

"I saw that," I say, then nod toward the bar. "You want a drink before we head upstairs?"

She shakes her head. "No, but an answer would be nice."

I grin wickedly, not even bothering trying to hide it as I take her hand, drawing her out of the bar toward the elevator, her jacket over her arm. "Why? Nervous?"

She laughs. "No. Should I be?"

"Liar," I whisper as the elevator doors close behind us and I draw her mouth toward mine. And damn, if she doesn't taste even better than she did two nights ago. She responds with a hunger that drives me wild, her arms wrapping around my neck as she boldly pulls me closer. She presses her curves against my chest with a soft moan, clearly wanting more, much more.

Taking lesson two slow is going to be a Herculean test of will, but I'm up for the challenge.

"Okay, so maybe I'm a little nervous," she murmurs as my lips roam over her jaw, finding the flesh of her earlobe. She's wearing little diamond earrings shaped like bow-ties, beautiful and delicate, just like her.

"Don't be." I take the entire lobe into my mouth, tasting the warmth of her perfumed skin melding with the cold stone of the gem for a moment before I set her free. "You're dressed for success."

She shivers lightly against me, her lips parting, but before she can speak, the doors open and she falls silent.

"Seriously, nothing to worry about," I assure her, wondering if I shouldn't have ambushed her the way I did the first time. But sooner or later, she's going to have to learn to take the wheel. Might as well begin as she'll need to continue.

"Let me tell you a secret," I say as I lead her down the hall. "A lot of men are terrified to make the first move. Even successful men used to taking control in the boardroom can falter in the bedroom."

CJ wrinkles her nose. "You? Falter in the bedroom?"

I laugh and scoff, "Well, no, not me. But the average guy. I've been thinking about how you came to be a twenty-five-year-old virgin, and it's not something that happened in a vacuum. I'm betting you scared a lot of men away."

She rolls her eyes. "Yes, because I'm soooo scary."

"You are," I assure her, pausing in front of the door to the suite. "You're drop-dead gorgeous, successful, and a little bit shy, so it can be hard to know what you're thinking. I'm sure that's a scary combo for a lot of guys."

Still looking dubious, she steps inside, taking in the elegant dining area to the left—complete with Tiffany chandelier—the seating area to the right, and the luxurious pedestal bed straight ahead. With its airy cotton drapes hanging from the ceiling, cloaking the mattress in mystery, it looks like something straight out of a castle. "So pretty . . ." She clasps her hands together, turning back to me with wide eyes. "This is too much, Graham."

"It's just enough. And you're going to look beautiful up on that bed."

Her eyes widen as I tip my chin toward the table, where a bottle of Dom is chilling in an ice bucket. "I have champagne if you've changed your mind about a drink."

"Now I'm worried," she says with a breathy laugh. "Is this lesson going to require liquid courage?"

I take her hand and bring her toe-to-toe with me. She gazes up at me, the heat that flickers in her expression assuring me she needs no liquid courage. "No. You've got this, Butterfly."

She gulps. "I do?"

"You do." I press a kiss to her forehead—knowing better than to kiss her lips if I want the strength to walk away from her, even for a few minutes—and turn to cross the room. I reach the throne-size, button-studded armchair, shift it to face her direction, and sit down, taking in the view. With her naughty heels and sexy-sweet dress, she's gorgeous. Knowing my lingerie is against her skin takes gorgeous to breathtaking.

I've never seen anything sexier in my life.

"Lesson two is about driving a man crazy and taking control of an erotic situation. Setting the mood, so to speak." I lean against the backrest, getting comfortable in the chair. "So, we're going to start with something no man can resist. A striptease from a beautiful woman."

CJ bursts into laughter, her head falling back before she shakes it, sending her ponytail flying from side to side. "Oh, no. No way. I can't."

"You can," I assure her. "And you will if you want to get an A in this class."

She bites her lip, her fingers tangling in front of her in a way that's both endearing and completely sexy. "But I really don't think I can, Graham. I've never done anything like that before. I'll make a fool of myself."

"No, you won't."

She snorts. "Yes, I—"

"No. You won't. Because I'm going to help you." I lift a finger, holding her gaze until she sighs heavily and gives a small nod, which I sense is the closest I'm going to get to enthusiasm at this point. "Start by lifting the hem of your dress. Slowly, taking your time. Owning the room."

She reaches for the bottom of her dress and immediately breaks into another round of laughter. She's gasping by the time she says, "I can't. Seriously, I can't."

"Caroline Jessica Murphy," I say in my best

displeased teacher voice. "Are you going to do as you're told, or am I going to have to turn you over my knee?"

She blinks once, twice, her eyes as round as the antique plates hanging on the wall behind her. "Are you serious?"

"Why?" I let my gaze track down her curves. "Would you like that? To have me spank you for being disobedient?"

Her eyes go even wider. "Um, I . . . I don't know. I'm not sure I would like that."

"But you aren't sure you wouldn't?" I arch a brow, heat surging to my groin.

She shakes her head and whispers, "No, I'm not sure about that, either. When you look at me like that, I can imagine liking all kinds of things I've never imagined liking before."

"Good." Her confession makes me even hotter. "Now, take off your dress for me, CJ. I want to see you in my lingerie."

She draws her lower lip between her teeth as she slowly reaches for the hem of the dress and then in one fluid motion pulls it up and over her head. And fuck me, but she's gorgeous. Heart-stopping. Even more beautiful than I thought she would be.

The blush-pink satin is so her, the crisscross fabric across the front suggestive and yet innocent at the same time. It's a hint of what's to come. A promise that if I'm very good, I can unhook the lingerie, let it fall to the floor, and admire her completely.

"When I saw that color, I knew it would look perfect against your skin. I knew it would make you feel so damn sensual. Does it, CJ? Does it make you feel beautiful? Alluring? Irresistible."

She nods, her lips parting, a soft little murmur falling from them. "All of that."

"Good. Because you are." My gaze drops to the matching garters that hold her stockings in place, and I groan. "So fucking irresistible." I motion to her hair. "Now your hair. I want it down."

"You want it down," she echoes, reaching both arms up to work the band from her hair, setting it free to fall in glossy waves around her shoulders. "You're a bossy one, aren't you?"

"I know what I want. And right now, I want you to untie the bow at the top of your corset," I say, my voice low and coaxing, daring her to own the moment. "Slow and confident, like you're unveiling a priceless, precious work of art."

Her breath hitches, but she obeys, pulling at the silk ribbon, making my pulse spike as she loosens the bow and her breasts spill over the top of the plunging neckline. My first glance is enough to make my heart stop. Her breasts are each a perfect creamy handful, graced by a dusky pink nipple. I'm dying to get my mouth on her, but not yet.

Not yet. Slow. Easy.

If I go too far, too fast, I'll scare her or hurt her, neither of which is an acceptable outcome.

Her hands cross above her chest as she whispers, "I'm embarrassed," proving she's misunderstood my silence.

"Oh no," I insist, shaking my head. "No, no, don't be. God, you're beautiful. I was just lost in thought."

"That can't be a good sign, if I'm taking my clothes off and you're lost in thought?"

"Thoughts about how much I want to get your nipples in my mouth," I say, desire thick in my voice. "How much I want to taste you. Every inch of you. You're driving me crazy, Butterfly, so please don't stop. Show me more of you. Torture me, slow and sweet."

Awareness flickers across her face, like the sun rising in the morning. Like the power of her sensuality is dawning on her at this moment. It's intoxicating to witness. It's a privilege to see her step into her sexual beauty.

"Torture . . ." she repeats.

"Exquisite torture," I add.

With slow, deliberate flicks of her fingers, she draws the ribbon through one eyelet and then another, loosening the corset until the last bit of ribbon slides free and the silk boning falls to the floor at her high-heeled feet, leaving her in nothing but the lace garter belt, matching panties, and thigh-high stockings.

"Good?" she asks, running a finger beneath the waist of the garter belt.

"So good," I murmur, my dick so hard there's no way she hasn't noticed the totem pole erected at the front of my pants. "Now the stockings."

Inch by inch, no, centimeter by centimeter—what an incredibly fast study she is when it comes to driving me out of my mind—she rolls the stockings down her toned thighs to the knee, then to her ankle, exposing more of her soft skin. I pull in a shaky breath, desperate to feel every inch of her bare beneath me, writhing and calling my name as I glide in and out of her tight heat.

She's crossed the line into goddess territory, and by the Mona Lisa smile on her face as she slowly turns her back, peeking at me over her shoulder as she grants me another killer view, I suspect she knows it.

"How do you feel about stripping now?" I ask. "Now that you've driven me out of my mind with wanting you?"

"Pretty good," she whispers with a nervous laugh. "But just FYI, I'm not going to be able to get the garter belt off in a sexy way. It's designed so that I have to take it on and off over my head, and it tends to get stuck on certain . . . obstacles."

I laugh, too, partly because the sound of her laughing is infectious. Maybe also because it can be fun to laugh even when you're burning with lust.

"Obstacles like your perfect tits?" My heart pounds as she wiggles out of the garter belt with her back to me, slaying me with every shift of her hips.

"You really think they're perfect?" she asks, freeing herself and tossing the belt to the floor as I make a mental note to consult with my design team for a garter fix.

"I do, but I'd like to feast my eyes on them again. Turn back to me. I've seen how gorgeous you look *in* the lingerie I make. Now I want to see how gorgeous you look out of it."

Slowly, carefully, she turns to face me, revealing nearly every stunning inch of her. She's ridiculously beautiful—the kind of angel fallen from the heavens men write poetry about. Innocence still flickers in her big eyes, making her all the more irresistible. She has no idea how dangerous she's becoming, how easy it would be for her to hold a man's soul in the palm of her hand.

Hell, I would sell mine in a heartbeat if that was what it took to ensure my mouth was on her skin in the next ten seconds. My cock jerks again, throbbing insistently in my pants, demanding to be allowed to attend the party.

Control. Must maintain control . . .

"You are the most beautiful thing I've ever seen," I say, my jaw clenched in an attempt to keep from scaring her, but my next words still emerge as a growl. *"Come. Here. Right now."*

She tosses her dark hair to the side again—God, she has a lot of hair, wild hair, all wavy and messy, the way I like it. "Now?" she asks, teasing me, apparently having no idea how close I am to the edge.

"Now," I repeat, my voice harsh. By the time she glides to a stop in front of me, my restraint is wearing thin. From the edge of my seat, I reach out and, almost violently, yank her close. The air whooshes out of her lungs as she braces her hands on my shoulders, setting her breasts to bobbing so near to my face it almost kills me.

"Did I really drive you crazy?" she breathes, excitement and surprise clear in her gaze as she meets mine. "You still look fairly calm."

I take her hand and plant it flush against my chest, covering it with my own. "Feel that?"

Her eyes widen as my heart does its best to jackhammer through my ribs. "Wow."

"Indeed," I agree, letting my gaze roam over every

inch of her. "Do I have permission to touch, Stripper Goddess CJ?"

"Oh, yes, please," she whispers, her fingers threading gently into my hair.

Carefully, I plant my hands on the backs of her thighs, drawing her closer then skimming my palms up over the ample curve of her ass. I can feel her tremble as I bend to kiss her belly, traveling to her navel, her hipbone.

"You taste like honey." I open my mouth, my tongue swirling into the hollow near her hip, wanting to lick every inch of her at once.

I lower my face to the top of her blush-pink panties, pressing a kiss to the fabric, inhaling her sexy scent as I do.

"Graham," she says my name so softly it barely registers.

"Yes, Butterfly?" I look up at her. Her brown eyes are fierce and strong, full of passion.

"There's a problem with my panties."

My brow knits. "What?"

"A big problem."

"These panties were tested six ways to Sunday by the design team." I shake my head. I can't conceive of what possible problem there would be. The fit, the feel— everything looks like it's made for her body. That's what my team does. They make beautiful lingerie that hugs the woman who wears it.

The flicker of a smirk spreads on her face. "That's not the problem."

CHAPTER 13

CJ

*H*e stares at me with worry in his blue eyes.

He's going to learn he has nothing to worry about.

And I'm about to experience something wholly new for me.

Stepping into the role of a seductress.

I lean closer to him, my breasts dangerously near his face, my lips moving closer to his ear. A thrill races through me at what I'm about to do, and I can barely hear him over the heartbeat pounding in my ears.

I'm not climbing a mountain or diving out of a plane, but to me this feels the same. I'm letting go of my safety harness and stepping into the sexual unknown. So far, he's directed me. He's told me what to do. I've cherished him taking the lead, and I want him to keep doing so.

But for a moment, I want to hold the reins.

My lips reach his earlobe, and I nip ever so gently on

it. He groans like an animal, and the sound electrifies me. "The problem is," I whisper, "that they're still on."

His breath hisses, and he grunts my name like it's a forbidden word. "CJ."

And then I take the next leap, telling him what I want. "Take them off," I whisper.

A growl is my reward, masculine and husky and so damn sexy. "You had me going, and look at you. You're teasing the teacher, and I fucking love it."

I want to shout *it worked, it worked*, but I'm too turned on to do anything but melt into his touch. I thought I was turned on the last time we were alone, but this is even more intense, like tiny electrical shocks are racing across my skin.

He hooks his fingers in the sides of my panties, and with a jerk, takes the reins again. I step out of the lingerie.

"Now spread your legs for me, Butterfly. Let me see you."

Flushed all over and dizzy with desire, I weave my fingers into his hair, holding onto him for support as I part my trembling legs, widening my stance, grateful that once again he's in charge.

"So sexy, so hot," he says, gazing hungrily at my newly exposed skin. Then, without warning, he leans over, flicking his tongue over the seam of me, and my knees go boneless.

God, how can one simple touch of his tongue be so intense?

I feel it everywhere, absolutely everywhere as he licks me again, teasing and probing, exploring me until I truly can't stand another moment. I gasp as my legs buckle.

"I've got you, baby." He catches me, easily lifting me into his arms and carrying me to the fairy-tale bed.

When he lays me down on the smooth white sheets, my pulse spikes, anxiety rearing its terrified head as he kneels between my legs and runs his warm hands down my thighs. I'm naked as the day I was born, and he's still fully dressed.

I blush at the inequity, my voice raspy as I ask, "What are you doing?"

"Finishing what I started," he says, his hands hooking behind my knees.

I know what he means, and I want it—oh, God, how I want it—but it feels even more intimate like this, lying down and stripped bare, with nothing to hide behind and nowhere to run if things get too intense. "I don't know if—"

"It's okay. *I* know," he says, slowly but surely spreading my legs wide. "And I need to make you come on my mouth, Butterfly. I need it like I need air."

Far be it from me to deny him breathing.

He lowers his face, kissing me there with such reverence my heart breaks a little. I never imagined it could be like this, that kinky things could be so unbearably sweet or filled with so much affection. That they could make me feel not just turned on, but cracked open, like a flower widening to the sun with no choice but to reach out and soak in the light it needs to stay alive.

But this might kill you. To have this and then lose it so fast...

For a moment, the thought is enough to scare away

the rush of pleasure, but then Graham moans and tilts his face, beginning to devour me with a single-minded intensity that leaves no doubt he loves everything he's doing to me, and I let go. I let go of worry and fear, and I give in to this, to this man who is everything I hoped he would be and so much more.

I fantasized about him when I was younger. But I never expected true pleasure could be this good, this transporting. I never knew he'd enjoy it so much, either, but judging from the sounds he's making as he devours me, we're both sliding into a new plane of bliss.

I relax into sensation, letting my knees fall wide open, threading my fingers through his hair. Pure pleasure radiates through me as his tongue laps me up. It's such an intoxicating mix of soft and filthy at the same damn time.

He slips his hands under my ass, pulling me to the edge of the bed and spreading me as his tongue glides across my wetness, up and down, then centering on my clit, where I ache for him. I ache exquisitely, and he knows just how to satisfy the need howling inside of me. He flicks his tongue, slow and deliberate, making my hips shoot up. Oh God, but I need more. More of him there, oh there, yes, *there* . . .

I rock into him, and he strokes faster, lavishing attention where I want him most, driving me into a fevered frenzy.

"Right there, oh yes, please, yes," I beg, gripping his hair more roughly, bringing him even closer as he sucks hard on my clit and the storm inside me intensifies.

My head thrashes from side to side, my hair flying into my face. "Oh, God, Graham. Oh, God," I gasp, and then I'm hurtling over the edge, coming with such force that it feels as if I'm tearing apart at the seams, shattering as my insides clench and release with a ferocity that is almost frightening.

I've always loved being scared. Only this isn't terrifying in the same way. This is wonderful and wicked, and it makes me feel so much more alive, like my entire body is plugged in, lit up and flickering with a million lights.

I run my hands through his hair, expecting him to slow his pace and stop, but he doesn't. He continues to consume me, his tongue pulsing deep inside, drawing out the exquisite release until I feel as if I'm having an out-of-body experience. Or perhaps another orgasm.

An unexpected second wave crashes over me, and I cry out. My vision blurs.

He slows his pace, pressing a final tender kiss to my center before he moves up.

"Oh . . . my . . . God," I pant, words becoming a hum of happiness as Graham rises over me and finds my lips with his, kissing me hard and deep. I taste myself on his tongue, but unexpectedly, I don't mind it. In fact, I almost *like* it. He tastes like he belongs to me, like *mine*.

Mine. Damn, but I like the sound of that way more than I should.

"That was amazing," I whisper, my voice dreamy. "Both."

"You're amazing. Multiplied," he says with a wink, then rolls onto his back in one swift motion. He pulls me on top of him, his hands cupping my ass as my thighs part and the thick ridge of his cock presses between my legs. Even through his pants, the sensation is enough to make me moan, low and hungry, in my throat.

I want that. I want *him*. I'm ready for every inch, no matter how much it might hurt, because being without him inside me hurts so much more.

"I'm ready," I say, as his hands travel over my ribcage and mold to my breasts. He guides one to his mouth, circling his tongue on my nipple until it draws even tighter, harder.

"Butterfly," he says, full of concern, "it's too soon. I don't want to rush you."

I shake my head hard, nearly coming out of my skin as he sucks my nipple into his mouth. "But that makes me want it even more."

He chuckles against my skin. "I love that you want it. And you have to know how badly I do, too. But I'd be a terrible teacher if I let the second lesson get too far out of control."

He lets go of my breasts and shoots me a sexy smile. *This man.* He knows how to make a woman want him, crave him, need him.

But it's more than all that. After only two lessons, I'm dying for him.

"I can't believe you have me this worked up already," I say softly.

"You worked up is my favorite dirty dream."

I nibble on the corner of my lips, thinking of my dirty dreams, and how he's starred in so many of them. How he's guiding me through the reality of them now. And once more I step into the sensuality that he's helping me see I possess.

"I have dirty dreams about you," I whisper.

He swallows. "You do?" The words come out like gravel.

I've surprised him again. Caught him off guard. And I like it.

Based on the pulsing shaft pressing into me, he likes it, too.

I nod. "I dream about stripping your clothes off." I'm not going to bother with finesse. But I like speaking my dirty mind with him. A dirty mind I always knew I had but was never able to put to good use until him.

He spreads his arms out wide on the bed, an invitation. "Then explore me, CJ. Take my clothes off like it's your dirty dream."

"Is this lesson three?"

A grin tells me he likes my impromptu plan. "Yes, it's lesson three. You're such a fast learner you deserve another session tonight."

He parks his hands behind his head.

Part of me can't believe this confident, cocky man wants a virgin to take his clothes off. But the look in his eyes says that's precisely what he wants.

Me.

I've turned him on.

I've aroused him.

I'm going to undress him.

Sparks race over my skin, and it's hard to imagine I can want him this much after coming twice.

But I'm learning all sorts of things are possible now that I'm visiting a country I've never traveled to before. One I very much want to spend a lot more time exploring.

I scoot back and tug his white dress shirt from his pants.

Graham has always looked good enough to eat, even clothed. I've feasted my eyes on him hundreds of times, but as my fingers open the small buttons of his crisp white shirt and spread it open, baring his chest, he literally takes my breath away.

He's the most gorgeous thing I've ever seen.

He has abs for days, and I trace the grooves of them with my fingertips. He shudders as I explore his flat belly, then again as I travel higher, my eager hands spreading over his firm, strong pecs. I sigh happily, certain now that I'm going to want to visit Graham Country many more times.

I let my fingers skim the line of hair from his navel to the smattering of darker, curlier hair across his chest, and murmur, "You're lovely."

"Like a butterfly?" he teases even as an almost pained expression crosses his face.

"Yes," I agree, laughing lightly. "Like a butterfly. A very manly butterfly."

I lean down to kiss him and end up nibbling on the skin of his abdomen the way he did mine. When I reach the close of his pants, I don't hesitate to pop open the top button, unzip his zipper, and pull them down over his hips. The movement draws his boxer briefs down, too, but I don't stop. I don't hesitate. I keep drawing the fabric lower until his erection springs free and the tips of my fingers go numb.

He's long and thick and just the right amount of veiny. His shaft pulses as I stare at him, my throat going dry. I gulp. It's beautiful, but *huge*, and I have no idea what I'm doing. Slowly, I reach out to touch the head, but my confidence drains away in a heartbeat. I don't know how to touch a man.

Graham, of course, notices. "You can stop," he says, through a clenched jaw. "It's okay."

Briefly, I consider stopping, letting that possibility play out. But that's an abhorrent thought. I don't want to stop. I want to *know*.

I raise my chin, calling on my inner tough girl, and my most honest self. "No. Just . . . show me how to touch you." My tongue slips out to wet my lips. "Teach me."

His eyes blaze with desire as he takes my hand and wraps it lightly around his thick shaft.

He groans at the same time that I gasp.

I murmur incoherent sounds in soft disbelief at how thick he is, how hard and heavy. At how desperately I can tell that he needs this. *My* touch.

That emboldens me.

I stroke him up and down, ending with a gentle squeeze, my eyes asking if it's okay.

Graham rewards me with a groan. "Fuck, yes. You got it, Butterfly. Just don't stop."

"Are you sure I'm doing it right?" I ask, needing the confirmation again, even though he's already given it.

He laughs lightly. "I'm positive." Then his laughter ends, and his eyes darken. "Do it again. Don't stop."

As I run my hand along his erection, a worry tugs at me. This man is so skilled in the bedroom. Am I going to put him to sleep with my tentative explorations? I run my fingers down the length of his cock to his balls. I touch them, very gently, feeling inadequate and wishing

I had done my research on how men like to have their balls played with.

"I'm not going to break," Grahams rasps out, his fingers gently encircling my arm. "Look at me, CJ."

I do, blowing the hair out of my face with pursed lips.

His eyes hold mine. His are fierce, honest, and a whole lot of hungry. "I promise you, there is nothing you can do that would be wrong. Nothing. You understand? That's the lesson, CJ. You're perfect as you are, and *your* touch drives me crazy."

"I want to do more than make you crazy," I say, my fingers tightening around his shaft. I take a breath, gathering up the guts to say what I want more than anything right now. "I want to make you feel as good as you make me feel. I want to make you come, Graham. For me. Because of me."

Cursing under his breath, he nods. "Do you fucking know how close I already am? I want nothing more than to come all over your hand."

His words light me up. Electricity races through my body, a wild thrill at the prospect of bringing him to the cliff and then over. It's dirty, it's erotic, and it's all so deliciously new. I want it desperately.

"How do you want me to touch you?" I ask.

He wraps his hand tighter around mine, guiding me up and down his length. Faster, rougher than I would on my own. "That's what you do. You keep going," he says, moving my hand even faster. "Up and down, not too hard, probably a little faster near the end. We're a lot less complicated than women."

"Easy sounds good to me right now."

"Trust me. You're making me look so fucking easy."

His playful words assuage my worries, and I draw in a breath. I can do this. I can absolutely do this. I grip him harder and follow his direction, stroking faster and rougher. He grits out my name in a twisted curse, and I feel a fresh wave of heat in my body.

"Butterfly?" he whispers.

"Yes?"

"Slide your hand between your legs, and bring some of that wetness to my cock."

Duh. Of course, he needs lube. Fortunately, I've got a more than ample supply thanks to the double dose of pleasure he gave me. I do as he asked then return my wet hand to his cock.

"Hey, look. It slides much easier," I say playfully as I demonstrate.

He smiles. "Yes, it does."

Then his smile falters, replaced by a look of intense concentration as I stroke him again. I pump him up and down, finding the rhythm that makes his breath come faster. A little more wetness, a little less friction, and he's rocking into my hand, thrusting his hips into my fist.

My breath catches and pleasure camps out in every cell in my body as I stare at the two of us, my hand on his hard-on. I'm wildly aroused from watching him, from doing this to him. His eyes squeeze shut, and I gaze at his throat, where the pulse seems to beat faster in his neck. His lips part, and he groans, louder than before. I've never heard anything so sexy in my life.

"That's it. A little faster."

I up the pace, gripping him even harder.

"*Yes. That,*" he says on a groan. "Coming."

I bite my lip, thrilled at the way his pleasure overtakes him, how he groans and thrusts, and then he's there, coming in my hand.

"Fuck," he mutters. Then he says it again and again. I'm not sure if I'm supposed to keep going at this tempo, but he seems to know I need his guidance, because he places his hand on mine, and slows my pace, even as he pants hard, coming down.

I let go, wash my hands, and return to his side. He presses a kiss to my forehead. "I haven't had a hand job in ages, and let me tell you, it was worth the wait. I don't think I've enjoyed an orgasm that much in years."

I beam. It's crazy to feel pride over a hand job, but I do. "I think it's safe to say I've never enjoyed giving one as much, either, and I loved every second of my first."

He laughs, drawing me in for another kiss. "I better clean up," he murmurs, kissing me once more before excusing himself.

When he returns, he slides in next to me. "Sleep with me," he murmurs, tugging me into the crook of his arm, and my heart skips a beat. Something stirs in my chest, a deeper feeling, a warmth that extends beyond what we did tonight.

"I would love to sleep with you," I say with a smile, and neither one of us misses the double meaning of the words, or the fact that tonight they mean something softer, more tender.

"You feel good, all nice and warm," he says in my ear, then presses a soft kiss to my neck.

"So do you." I settle in next to him, sighing happily as

he spoons me. "Is this another lesson? Are we squeezing in lesson four?"

"How to cuddle after a fantastic orgasm," he murmurs.

"Now *that* I think I'll excel at."

But he shakes his head against my hair. "It's not a lesson."

"It's not?"

He brushes my hair away from my skin, his touch gentle. "Nope. It's just what I want more than anything right now."

That feeling in my chest? It intensifies. It multiplies. It soars. It's almost better than my double Os. I let myself feel it for a few seconds before I return to the task of keeping my head and heart separate.

But separate doesn't mean resisting a good snuggle. I cuddle against him, savoring the heat from his body, my thoughts drifting into sleepy pastures.

Until my phone howls in my purse.

Literally *howls*, the full-moon baying of wolves that means there is serious trouble at home. My landlord never calls unless there is a bona fide emergency, the kind that cannot wait until morning.

"Don't answer that," Graham murmurs. "I'm about to have a fantastic dream about you falling asleep in my arms."

"I was going to have the same dream. But I have to grab this call."

I hit the green button and bring the phone to my ear, where my "Hello?" is met by an endless stream of cursing in Czechoslovakian. But in between all the cursing, I catch a few key words—*broken pipes, ruined carpet*, *structural damage*, *damned cat*, and *loose in the building*.

With a silent groan of abject misery, I promise to be there as soon as I can, to clean everything up and pay for all damages, and to get my renegade pussycat back in his cage ASAP.

I love that little guy. God, how I love him.

But right now, I wish my brother had owned a pet rock.

CHAPTER 14

GRAHAM

The entire way to the Meatpacking District in the cab, all I can think about is muzzles. Surely they have cat muzzles, right? Something snappy-looking but secure that CJ can wrap around her cat's destructive mouth before she leaves the house. I mean, I get that Stephen King is old and blind and easily confused about what is food and what isn't, but right now, I would have zero issues with muzzling the fluffy bastard.

And I wasn't even cock-blocked by the stupid cat.

I was . . . snuggle-stonewalled. Cuddle-confounded. Spoon-stymied.

Jesus. What's wrong with me? I'm pissed at a senile old feline because I didn't get to curl up and slip into the land of nod with the loveliest woman ever?

I look in the rearview mirror, answering my own question.

Yes. Evidently, yes.

"You don't have to come up. You can wait out front

if you don't want to deal, or if you want to answer emails or whatever," CJ says, bolting from the cab as soon as I've passed a twenty through the hole in the glass. "It's going to be ugly. And wet. And there's probably going to be a lot of yelling. My landlord isn't happy."

"And why should he be?" As soon as she turns her key, I follow her through the front door and toward the third floor. "Your pet wreaked havoc on his property."

"No, *I* wreaked havoc on his property when I forgot to put the baby lock back on the kitchen cabinet," she says, huffing as she hurries around the first-floor landing. "Stephen King can't help it. He suffers from dementia, and dementia increases his stress levels, and increased stress levels make him want to chew things."

"Nothing a muzzle won't cure," I mutter under my breath.

CJ frowns at me over her shoulder but doesn't stop climbing. "I heard that. And I'm not going to muzzle him. I believe in letting creatures age with dignity. Especially creatures who I happen to love, and who I don't want to see wander out into the street and get run over."

The reminder of how much she adores this crazy old cat sends the frustration in my chest rushing away, banished by the vulnerability in her voice.

"I'm sorry. And don't worry. We're going to find Steve. And he's not going to get run over. Not on my watch."

Yep. I'm Ed Harris, guiding the astronauts safely home from a failed moon mission in *Apollo 13*, delivering his brazen vow: *We've never lost an American in space, we're sure as hell not gonna lose one on my watch!*

Cat-retrieval failure is not an option.

The time for honor is upon me. It's my duty to help the woman find her feline.

As we reach the third floor and speed-walk toward the sound of Slavic cursing at the end of the hall, CJ reaches out, giving my hand a quick squeeze. "Let me handle Arno, okay? He sounds scary, but he can be reasoned with. Usually. Sometimes."

Before I can respond, or suggest that maybe she should go look for the cat while I soothe Arno's rage with a few crisp one hundred dollar bills, CJ darts through the door to her apartment and into the heart of the chaos.

Arno, a balding man with rheumy blue eyes and too-pink features, gesticulates wildly at CJ and the heavens and hell, and everything in between, but my gut tells me he's not a threat. He's angry, yes, but harmless. The real danger is coming from under the sink. Water is gushing out of the cabinet and onto the already soaked carpet, where a stain the size of a small elephant is growing larger every second. It's completely saturated. If water hasn't soaked through to the subfloor yet, it will soon, and then this repair is going to go from expensive to sky-high.

I have no idea why Arno hasn't turned the damn water off, but if he's too busy yelling to take care of business, I have no problem doing it for him.

Picking my way around the chunks of mauled potato and onion littering the floor—it looks like Stephen King snacked on a few other things, besides piping—I squish through the soaked carpet, kneel down, and reach beneath the sink. The hot water knob sticks, but eventually gives with a squeal, and in just a few seconds I have both the hot and cold water shut off at the source and the situation relatively under control.

As soon as the water stops gushing, the flood of cursing ceases.

"How do you do?" Arno asks in a thick accent.

I turn to see him motioning toward the sink and figure he isn't actually inquiring about the state of my health. "I shut it off at the source. The valves are under the sink."

His pale brows furrow as he blinks. "Under sink?"

I nod, trying to keep my voice judgment-free. "Yep. Right there. Under the sink, just turn them all the way to the right. And I'm guessing it's the same set-up in every unit, so you'll know next time you have a problem."

He grunts, seemingly impressed, and I silently wonder how a man can be a damned landlord—or an adult, for God's sake—and not know how to shut off water to the sink. But this is the same man who thought it was acceptable to install all-over shag carpeting in the unit, even in the kitchen, so he's clearly not in the habit of tackling apartment issues properly.

"Thank you, Graham," CJ says, beaming at me like I just saved a baby from a burning building. And though I know I did nothing even close, I can't deny it feels good to be looked at like that. Especially by her, this woman who is all I think about lately, all I dream about.

She claps her hands together and adds in an upbeat

voice, "Now we just need to find Stephen and get this cleaned up and—"

"No, you out." Arno's chest puffs as his arms flail toward the door.

CJ's face goes white. "Oh, no. Please, Arno, I promise nothing like this will ever happen again. I'll lock the child safety locks every time. Please, I love living here, and I've never been late with my rent, not once in three years. Can't we—?"

"No, no, not out for good," Arno says, his bluster softening in the face of CJ's pleading. "Out for week. To fix carpet and floor and to make tile. We make tile here now so easier to clean."

CJ nods quickly. "Oh, yes! That would be wonderful. The shag was hard to keep clean, if I'm being completely honest. And I'm happy to cover the tile costs."

"You'll do no such thing." I wade back across the soaked carpet, water oozing in through my shoes to dampen my socks. "The guy who redid my bathroom last year is amazing, and he owes me a favor. I'll get in touch with him tomorrow morning and get a crew over to clean up the water ASAP. Hopefully we can have this all dried up and tiled by next week. My treat." I extend a hand to Arno. "Agreed?"

"You pay bill?" He cocks his head, studying me out of the corner of his eyes. "All bill? Whole bill?"

"Every dime," I assure him.

"And you pick nice color," he adds, pointing at my chest. "Nothing too crazy. No pink."

"No pink," I agree drily. "It will be tasteful and of the highest quality."

With his lip curling in apparent satisfaction, Arno nods and clasps my hand, pumping my arm up and down. "Good. Done." He releases my palm and points his stubby finger in CJ's direction. "You find cat. You take him out. I let work crews into apartment and make sure valuables are safe. No worries."

CJ presses her hands together. "Thank you so much, Arno. Thank you."

Grumbling and nodding, Arno waves away her thanks and shuffles stiffly across the room. A moment later, CJ and I are alone with the soaked floor, the potato and onion chunks, and the smell of wet carpet, which is better than wet dog, but not by much.

"Thank you," she says. "I appreciate the sweet offer, but I insist on paying for the work and the clean-up."

I shake my head as I reach out, pulling her in for a hug. "Not a chance, Murphy. I've got this covered. Consider it an early birthday present."

"I can't let you do that."

Failure is not an option tonight. That applies, too, to my offer to pay. Given the uncharitable thoughts that just coursed through my head about her poor cat, I *need* to pay. It's only right. "Butterfly, this is not up for negotiation. I'm paying for it. It's that simple."

She pulls back from the embrace to stare at me, searching my eyes, like she can find an answer there. "You've already done so much for me."

"And you've done so much for me." As the words emerge, I realize how true they are. We've only spent a few nights together, and they've not only been insanely sexy, but fun and tender, too. More than I expected. "I intend to pay."

She softens. "You're so chivalrous."

It comes out the same way she said I was lovely earlier, and it does funny things to my chest. "That's me. Graham Chivalrous Campbell."

"That means I'm paying for birthday brunch this year. No arguments." Her arms go around my waist as her cheek rests on my chest, sending a wave of pure contentment washing through me. This night certainly isn't proceeding the way I thought it would—I was sure I'd be dreaming dirty dreams while she dozed in my arms—but somehow, it's okay. It feels like about anything would be okay, or at least survivable, as long as I get to hug CJ after it's over. She just feels so good, so right.

"I guess we should get hunting for this wayward kitty," I say, pressing a kiss to the top of her head because I can't help but touch her. "Any idea where he might have gone?"

CJ tips her head back, gazing up at me with a crooked smile. "I have a few ideas, but you're not going to like them. When he freaks out, he tends to hide in the darkest, dustiest places he can find. Once, I found him behind the furnace. Another time, he wedged himself behind the toilet."

I frown. "Are you implying that I'm a squeamish man who won't brave the elements on a rescue mission?"

She laughs. "No, you're a very manly man who knows how to turn off water and has a tile guy on speed dial. But you're also wearing very expensive pants."

"Forget my pants. Let's get that cat and get out of here. I would like to get you back in bed sometime before midnight, Miss Murphy. I was enjoying spooning you very much, but I also think I'll enjoy sliding my hand between your legs in the middle of the night."

Heat flashes in her eyes. "I would like that, too."

"Maybe even a refresher on lesson one or two?"

Her eyes darken, a hint of desire flickering in them. "Extra credit is good."

I chuckle and smack her rear, hauling her close for a hot second and planting a kiss on those soft, delicious lips. "You'll get lots of homework, I promise."

Then I let her go because it's kitty-cat time. "Let's go kitty hunting."

We start with her apartment, but unsurprisingly, there's no sign of Steve. But with the amount of screaming that went on in here tonight, I wouldn't have expected an anxious animal to stick around. A thorough search of the hallways and common areas comes next. We scour the stroller storage and the janitor's closet on the first floor, where snow shovels and mildew-scented mops crowd in the darkness, but there are no signs of fuzzy feet or a twitching tail.

Down in the basement, we pace every inch of the boiler room, using our phones for light as we poke into windowless rooms that clearly haven't been touched—or cleaned—in the past century.

"If there isn't black mold down here, I'll eat my own hand," I mutter as we finish another horror-movie-worthy exploration.

"Don't eat your hand," CJ says, with a yawn. "I like your hand. Your hand does nice things to me. Maybe even in the middle of the night."

I wrap my arm around her waist with a sigh,

knowing the chances of getting my hands back on her later are diminishing with every passing minute. "Where to next?"

"The courtyard, I guess." She starts up the stairs in front of me, granting me a killer view of the hem of her dress swishing temptingly against the backs of her thighs. Lord have mercy . . .

"Have I mentioned how much I love this dress?"

She reaches the top of the stairs and turns to smile at me, her wild hair backlit by the orange glow of the lobby light. "No, you haven't. But thank you."

I shake my head, too struck by the beauty of that smile to reply. Damn, she's pretty. And sweet. And so much fun to be with that I'm actually enjoying this stupid cat hunt. At least a little bit.

Though by the time we search the courtyard—crawling on our hands and knees to peek under every bit of decorative stonework large enough to hide Stevie —my pants are ruined, my bones are starting to ache, and I'm so tired all I want to do is curl up in the pink playhouse by the playground equipment and go to sleep.

"You checked the playhouse?" I ask, fighting to suppress yet another yawn.

"Yes. Twice." CJ yawns eloquently before hitting a button on her phone with a sigh. "It's almost two o'clock. If we don't find him in the next few minutes, I want you to go back to the hotel, or your place, without me. Get some rest."

"And what will you do?"

"I'll stay here and look." She shrugs, her hands lifting helplessly at her sides. "I mean, I can't give up. He has to be somewhere. I know he didn't leave the building. He wouldn't do that, right? Even if someone held open the door to the outside world? He wouldn't run off into the city, because if he did, I'd never find him, and he'd definitely get run over."

With my heart aching for her, I pull her close, rocking her gently from side to side. "I'm staying. Until the bitter end. Until every soldier is brought in from the field of battle."

She hums into my shirt, sagging against me. Then she lifts her head—sharp and sudden. "That's it." She steps out of my arms, turning to face the playground equipment. "The field of battle . . ."

I frown. "The slide?"

"The kids play knights and dragons out here all the time," she says, moving toward the swing set. "And they're always dropping their toys and their snacks. And Steve's nose still works pretty well, considering the state the rest of him is in . . ." As she reaches the structure, she falls to her knees, scraping the wood chips away until she gets a clear view beneath the blue tunnel running from one section of the equipment to the other.

Her cry of victory is one of the sweetest sounds I've heard tonight. "There you are! Stevie, baby, come here. Oh, poor pumpkin, you must be so scared."

When she stands, there's a giant, fluffy Himalayan with wrinkled whiskers, a freckled nose, and soft blue eyes snuggled into her arms.

"Stephen King, good to see you again." I lean down to get a better look at him in the dim glow of the motion-activated lights illuminating the yard. "You're a handsome old gent, I'll give you that."

The cat meows, as if returning the compliment, and CJ giggles. "He is. I'm a sucker for a pretty face. And a sweet spirit." She hugs him closer. "Come on, love, off to the vet for you. You can visit with Dr. Miller while we get the house cleaned up."

By the time we get Steve into his cat carrier, gather his food, pack CJ's bags for a week out of her apartment, and deliver the cat to the 24-hour vet, it's three thirty in the morning.

A huge yawn escapes me as we stand outside the vet's office.

She joins me in the yawn parade. "If it's okay, I think I'll go crash at the hotel until morning. Then, since I don't have a place to stay for the week, I can look for an apartment rental or something tomorrow when I'm not fried."

But there's no need to return to the St. Regis. I have a better idea. "Come home with me. We could both use some sleep, and my bed is sinfully comfortable."

"Are you sure?"

I scoff. "I'm not sending you to the St. Regis solo, and my place is closer. We aren't done with our non-lesson of cuddling, my butterfly. Besides, we only have a few more nights of classes, and I want to make the most of my time with you. Although, of course, I want you to feel free to stay at my place even after the board meeting, until your apartment is fixed. I have more than enough space, and I'm happy to have you."

She stiffens briefly in my arms, and I fear I've said the wrong thing.

"Right? Do you want to make the most of this?" I ask, tucking a finger under her chin and raising her face so she can meet my eyes.

A flicker of sadness colors her expression—maybe she hates being away from her home base as much as I do—but then it's gone, replaced by a certainty. "Yes. Yes, I do."

An Uber ride later, we drag our exhausted bodies into my place and take care of our pre-bed business. I'm the first to collapse onto my king-size mattress. She slides on a T-shirt that says *When I think about books I touch my shelf,* and the sight of it on her—a naughty little bookworm—makes me laugh. "So very you," I say, and she curtsies and gets into bed with me.

As we snuggle under the covers, that "just right" feeling returns.

When this evening started, I pictured it ending with a departure from the St. Regis before dawn, well before CJ wound up tangled up in my arms.

But now that I have her here, it's the perfect end to her stripping.

Just for me.

Only for me.

It's so good that I drift off to sleep with the sweet smell of CJ filling my head and dream the nicest dreams I can remember having in ages.

But the next morning, as so often happens with sweet dreams, there's a nightmare just around the corner. Waiting in my lobby. Dressed in a hot-pink raincoat and stiletto heels.

CHAPTER 15

CJ

*B*est. Sleepover. Ever.

Spending the night with Graham was never on my sex ed agenda—I figured that belonged in a relationship class rather than a seduction course—but now I can't imagine my lesson plan being complete without this extra session. Drifting off in his arms, waking up with his lips warm on my neck and his husky voice asking if I want coffee, meeting his eyes in the mirror as he shaved and I swept on a coat of mascara—it was all wonderful. Perfect. A lesson in intimacy and the "morning after" that I won't soon forget.

Because I'll be repeating it tonight.

And the next night, and the next, and the next.

Then I'll be moving into his guest room . . . I guess. Once the seven days of sex-cation are over, and if my apartment is still under construction . . .

I knew from the start that we had an expiration date, but when Graham said that last night, about me staying past Monday since he has plenty of room, it hurt a little.

I didn't realize how upsetting it would be to imagine a future without his kiss, his touch, or the new closeness that's growing between us. I'm seeing sides of Graham I never knew were there, and experiencing the pleasure of his company in ways that go beyond the physical.

Though that's quite nice, too. If "nice" means absolutely toe-curlingly incredible.

I'm daydreaming about everything we did to each other last night—about the moment when I made him lose control in my hand, and how much I want to do that again—when we step out of the elevator into the lobby. Graham stops dead, cursing softly beneath his breath.

I follow his mildly horrified gaze to a leggy woman posed near the front desk. Everything from her hot-pink raincoat, skin-tight pink skirt, scandalously low-cut gray blouse, and sky-high stilettos screams, "Look at me!" Add in the bouncy blond hair and expertly made-up blue eyes, and she's probably one of the prettiest people I've ever seen in real life.

But there's something . . . not right about her smile, something that reminds me of what it feels like to be the last kid picked for volleyball in gym class every single day.

Anything with balls, I'm bad at. Which reminds me . . .

Note to self: research how to correctly play with a man's balls so you have something new to show Graham tonight.

"Hey, G-man," the woman purrs, eliminating any doubt that she's exactly what she looks like—one of Graham's women. I've only met a few of his former girl-friends, usually in passing at a reception or event, and they've all been stunning to the point where other women feel like trolls in comparison.

"Lucy." Graham's voice is clipped, brimming with irritation. I glance up at him, my eyes wide.

So this is the woman Graham said turned stalker on him after their breakup a few months ago.

Ouch.

I glance back at her, trying to hide my knowledge of her past misdeeds—who buys an ex-lover a plane ticket to Barbados or takes up running solely for the opportunity of bumping into him on his morning jog, for goodness' sake? Running is abhorrent. But I school my expression, keeping my face neutral, since I don't want her to feel embarrassed. I'd be deeply embarrassed if I knew an ex of mine had been talking about me with his new lover.

"Hey, I know this is kind of out of the blue." Lucy's eyes flit from Graham to me and back again with a nervous laugh. "And I'm sorry to, um, interrupt your morning. I just, I think I left my scarf at your place. You know, the black silk I always wear with this outfit?"

She motions down at her décolletage—which is impressive, borderline inappropriate if she's on her way to the office, and could definitely benefit from a scarf tied at the neck to help conceal some of the extra boobage going on—but Graham's eyes remain fixed firmly on her face.

"I don't have anything of yours in my apartment, Lucy," he grinds out through a tight jaw. "It's all gone, and I would appreciate it if you would honor the boundaries we talked about."

Her brows pinch. "I know you said I shouldn't come

over," Lucy says, her voice creeping half an octave higher. "But I was just a couple blocks away and I thought—"

"Think again next time," Graham says. "You should know by now I don't say things I don't mean. So I would appreciate it if you would take me at my word. Like when I texted you the other day, and asked you to stop contacting me. I meant it."

Hurt flashes across Lucy's features, her emotional pain so obvious, I can't help but flinch in empathy. God, this poor woman. She's a wreck. Like a very beautiful, well-put-together addict hunting for a fix she's never going to be able to lay her hands on again, no matter how finely she dresses or how hard she tries.

The thought sweeps through my head followed by an eerily clear mental image of me standing where Lucy is now, clutching my suitcase and thanking Graham for a great seven days, when all I really want to do is cling to his leg and beg him to let me stay a little longer.

Maybe a lot longer.

My stomach churns at the thought. This is precisely what I promised myself I'd avoid. This is what I've been determined to keep at bay.

Lucy apologizes softly, her eyes shining with tears, and as she hurries toward the door, I realize how easy it would be to get hooked on Graham. Hooked just as *hard*. I already crave his touch, ache for his laughter, yearn to be wrapped up in his arms at the end of the night and wake there in the morning.

"Sorry about that," Graham murmurs, lifting a hand to the man behind the lobby desk as we move toward the revolving doors. "She doesn't seem to be getting the message that it's over."

I force a sympathetic smile. "Well, hopefully she will now. You were pretty firm."

He grunts. "I have to be firm. I was pretty damn clear the other day, too. We moved past the let-her-down-easy phase a long time ago."

"I get it," I say, though of course I don't. I've never had that kind of relationship before, the kind that leaves you so desperate you'll keep rolling over and showing your vulnerable underbelly, no matter how many times you're kicked to the curb. I cringe at the thought, and the stark realization that I don't want to experience that kind of devastation. I don't want to become Lucy. "See you tonight?"

"Tonight." Graham leans down to kiss the top of my head. "I'll be home by six thirty. I'm going to skip the run today."

"Same here. I'm too beat for biking. I'll probably be back around six thirty as well. Thanks for letting me stay."

"Letting you stay." He chuckles as we emerge into the cool spring morning and he starts toward the town car parked at the corner. "You say that as if it's some sacrifice on my part. You know I wouldn't have it any other way." He pauses, jabbing a thumb over his shoulder as his brow furrows. "Do you need a ride? We can swing by your office first. It's no trouble at all."

I wave a hand and continue backing toward Chelsea, buttoning my jacket. "No, it's fine. I want to walk. It's not far, and I do my best brainstorming while walking."

"Are you sure?" He narrows his eyes with a smile,

looking so handsome, so tempting, that I almost reverse direction and hurry into the car beside him.

But in the end, I shake my head and wave. "I'm sure. Have a great day."

I need to walk, to think about the work ahead and what to tackle on my agenda. The cool air usually helps clear my head. But by the time I reach the door to the space Love Cycle shares with several other up-and-coming designers, I've barely been able to think about sample shots or inventory. All I can think about is Graham, and how deep into the water I've waded with him already, so deep I can barely keep my head above the surface.

It would be dangerous to tread any deeper. My gut is issuing a red alert, and my heart is hammering out a *careful, careful, be careful* rhythm that makes it impossible to focus on my to-do list.

I know what I need to do. As soon as I reach my desk, I lock myself in my office and search for a hotel room for the next week.

CHAPTER 16

*M*y phone bleats with a code red text.

That's Luna speak for a massive shopping emergency.

Even though I have a shit ton of work on my desk, I won't ignore my friend. I call her while tapping out the last line of an email to our design team, approving the quick garter fix they worked up this morning. "Talk to me."

"I'm stuck." It comes out in a long, needy whine, and I strain to make out the sounds behind her, the clicking of shoes, a few *can I help yous*, the ding of an intercom.

In my best stay-calm voice I say, "Tell me where you are. Are you stuck in the linen department at Bloomingdales again? Are you rocking in a corner yet, or are you still upright and semi-functional?"

She chokes out several miserable-sounding sobs. "Yes. Bloomingdales. Upright. But just barely. Shopping is so awful. How do you people manage this?"

"By 'people' do you mean men?"

"Everyone. Men, women, children. This is the worst. I can't do it, Graham. *Help me, Obi Wan Kenobi. You're my only hope.*"

"When you put it like that . . ." I glance at the clock. Fortunately, Bloomingdale's is close. "Tell me what department you're in. Try to describe it. I'll be there in ten minutes to perform a search-and-rescue."

"There are things for the home. Like cake dishes, and ice cream scoops, and blenders. Does that mean I'm in hell? Because they aren't selling ice cream and cake, so it sounds like hell."

"Stay there. I'll find you in housewares."

I hang up, and head to the elevator. Luna's being dramatic, of course. She knows how to navigate her way out of Bloomingdale's. But she detests shopping with the force of a thousand suns, and since I happen to be a master at picking the right item for the right person, I see it as my personal duty to lend a helping hand.

I find her holding a stainless steel elephant napkin holder in one hand and a miniature purple hammer in the other, staring back and forth at each, those cat-eye glasses low on her nose. A huge purse is slung on her shoulder.

When I reach her, I pat her on the back. "Breathe."

She takes a deep breath, and I remove each item from her hands, setting them down at their displays. "Luna, no one wants an elephant napkin ring for a gift, and I assure you, as cute and kitschy as this hammer is, no one actually needs it."

She blinks up at me. "Yes, you're right."

"Tell me who you're shopping for. And why you

didn't call me first. We've been over this. You're not supposed to go into the big department stores by your-self," I tease, talking to her like a child.

She squares her shoulders. "I wanted to get some-thing nice for Valerie because she's had a rough week at work, and the other night she mentioned something about how nice the table looked when it was set all fancy at a restaurant. So, naturally, I thought she wanted napkin rings."

I shake my head in sympathy and pet her hair. "Sweetheart, I assure you, no one ever wants napkin rings. If Valerie had a hard week at work, there's only one thing you can give her."

"Graham, I did that last night." She wiggles her eyebrows. "Twice."

"Shut your filthy mind off and go get your wife a gift certificate for a spa day."

Her eyes sparkle, and she snaps her fingers. "You *are* the king of gift giving."

I blow on my fingers, the sign for too-hot-to-handle.

"That's exactly what I need to do." Her smile is infectious.

"And look, there's a great spa around the corner. Stellar Spa. Some of the ladies at the office rave about it. You go there and get a day of pampering for your woman."

She grabs my cheeks and plants a kiss on my fore-head. "I love you." She's about to turn around when she says, "Hey, how are things going with your lesson plans?"

I don't bother to hide the smile that tugs at my lips. "They're going great."

"And she's a good student?"

I let that word roll around in my brain for a moment. *Student.* CJ hardly feels like a student. She feels like so much more. But "more" is precisely what I need to be on guard against. *More* can distract me from my mission—to laser in on growing Adored.

"The classes are mutually enjoyable."

She laughs, shaking her head. "I'd badger you for more details if I wasn't in a rush. Oh, by the way." She dips her hand into her cavernous bag and hands me a small, white bakery box. "A whoopie pie for you."

I tilt my head to the side. "Luna, did you know you were going to call me from Bloomingdale's before you walked through the revolving door?"

She shrugs sheepishly. "I might have preplanned a baked bribe."

"I'll always accept your baked goods, bribe or not." I make a shooing gesture. "Now get your ass to Stellar Spa."

With an afternoon snack in hand, I leave the store. Once outside, my phone buzzes with a note from CJ that stops me in my tracks.

For a full five seconds.

Then I charge into the nearest coffee shop, one next door to a florist, set the whoopie pie down, and get to work on this new crisis.

CHAPTER 17

CJ

*M*y heart wages war with my brain, but no way am I letting that *tra la la* organ win this battle.

Booking a hotel is the sensible action to take.

Informing Graham is the adult thing to do.

I will be both sensible and adult. With the web page for the Warwick Hotel open on my laptop, ready and waiting for me to finish reserving a room, I tap out a note.

CJ: Thank you again for the offer to stay at your place. I'm so grateful, but I've decided I should stay at a hotel. I don't want to cramp your style, and sleeping over night after night was never part of our bargain.

GRAHAM: Part of the bargain? That's not what this is about. I don't want you to stay with me as part of a bargain. I want you to stay with me because I like having you with me. And for the record, you aren't cramping my anything. Is this because of Lucy?

"No," I mutter to myself. "Not in the way you think, anyway."

There's no way Graham can know how Lucy has made me realize how vulnerable my heart is. Not to mention my sanity. Graham literally makes women crazy with wanting him, and I don't need crazy in my life. I like peace, harmony, and routine, thank you very much. I get more than enough crazy dealing with twenty employees and an out-of-state production and warehouse situation.

I decide to lean on a little humor.

CJ: I don't think multiple sleepovers are in the sex education curriculum.

GRAHAM: Multiple orgasms are, though, and they're aided by multiple sleepovers. Plus, last time I checked, I was the teacher. And the teacher would like his model student in his bed.

SINCE HUMOR ISN'T WORKING, I'll need to break out the big guns. I gulp. Time to be direct.

CJ: You are, but I don't need to learn how to be a considerate houseguest. I know how to do that. And in this situation, that means I should stay in a hotel.

HE DOESN'T REPLY RIGHT AWAY, and I set my phone down to focus on work, then it buzzes again with a text.

GRAHAM: This isn't about being a houseguest. This isn't about politeness, CJ. This is something else, since I'm pretty sure until my ex showed up that you enjoyed spending the night with me, too. It's over with her. It's history. And I truly want you to stay with me. So what is it going to take for you to give me another chance to convince you? I'd really like to fall asleep with you again, and wake up with you, and do everything in between.

I'M STARTING to type a reply when my phone rings. His name is big and bold. Demanding. Like him.

And damn it, I like his demands, which is part of the problem.

"Hello, Graham," I say, playing it cool. I love that he's calling to plead his case—it makes me feel special—but I truly intend to book that room.

"Butterfly." His tone is firm, a little commanding, a lot sexy.

"Yes?"

"You are one tough woman, and it sounds like your

mind is made up. But I can be pretty persuasive. Give me twenty minutes to change your mind."

A shiver runs through me. Is he suggesting some afternoon delight? The idea is, well . . . a whole lot more than delightful. "Are you saying you'd like to pop over to my office and—"

"—bend you over your desk and remind you why you want to stay at my place?"

The shiver turns into a pulse, beating low and hot in my belly. Still, I try my best to think rationally. "Graham, this isn't about sex or lessons."

"I know, Butterfly. Trust me. And that's precisely why I'm *not* coming to your office to bend you over the desk. Nor to spread you out in front of me and devour your sweet pussy." His voice is husky, and a small gasp escapes my lips at his words. "I'm not going to shut the door to your office or kiss you until you melt for me the way you did the first night, the way you do every night. Even though I want that. *Badly.*"

I grip the edge of my desk, tingles spreading like wildfire across my skin. God, I want that badly, too. *Must. Stay. Strong.*

"So what *are* you going to do?" I ask evenly.

"Just wait. You'll have the answer in twenty minutes."

He hangs up.

I shake my head, trying to rid it of thoughts of that man. The trouble is, he seems dead-set on convincing me, and judging from the flush flooding my cheeks, my body wants to be convinced. But I need to stick to my plan. Batten down the hatches. Time to be an iron butterfly without a single soft spot in my armor.

On impulse, I reach out, punching the intercom and

calling my intern. "Katie, could you grab me one of those green smoothies from the market downstairs? The kind with extra kale and seaweed?"

"Gross," Katie pipes back, proving I've done an excellent job of making her feel comfortable here, despite the fact that she's the only team member under twenty-one. "But will do, boss. You want an iced coffee, too? To wash out the nasty taste after the green thing?"

I hesitate only a moment before giving in. "Yes, Katie. Please. That sounds perfect."

And it does. I will build up my fortitude with green superfoods, caffeinate myself to brimming-with-confidence levels, and then stand firm against Graham's superpowers of persuasion. There's nothing he can do to convince me.

Twenty minutes later, Katie knocks on my door.

"Come in."

When she opens it, she's carrying a massive bouquet of flowers. Bright orange, sunshine yellow, fiery flowers. Her face is hidden behind three—wait, no, *four* dozen tiger lilies.

I don't recall telling him I loved tiger lilies.

But then I remember our phone call a few nights ago. I mentioned them briefly, simply in passing.

The man knows how to listen. He pays attention. He cares.

Talk about a superpower.

Fighting off a massive grin, I take the flowers and set them on my desk.

"These, obviously, are for you," Katie deadpans. "Based on the sheer number, some guy either needs to make up or convince you to be his, and if you say no, I'll say yes because a man who sends four dozen flowers is a keeper."

The smile won't disappear. "Thank you, Katie."

She hands me the card. With nervous fingers, I open it.

Stay with me.

Katie clears her throat. "Um, there's more."

"More?"

She thrusts a white box at me. The sticker reads *Luna's Sweets.* Inside is a delectable-looking whoopie pie. I haven't had one of these in ages, and it smells delicious. There's a note here, too. A longer one.

I made dinner reservations at eight. I'm taking you out to your favorite restaurant. But feel free to have dessert first. These whoopie pies are irresistible. Just like you.

The grin? It consumes all of me. Not just my face. I swear it's a full-body smile.

Katie clears her throat. "I have your kale smoothie and the coffee. Do you still want them?"

I shake my head. "No. I don't need them anymore."

I don't need fortification because I don't want to resist him.

Because I'm beginning to understand that he's not the only teacher around here. I'm teaching myself, too, pushing myself to step out of my comfort zone and grow. And the lesson I have mapped out for CJ Murphy for the next few nights is this—learn to enjoy myself with a man without falling head over heels and losing my grip on my sanity.

I will savor this whoopie pie, I will savor the whoopee, and then I will walk away from both with my head held high.

CHAPTER 18

CJ

*B*y the end of the day, I'm so hyped up on sugar and anticipation that I decide to hit the gym after all. I would rather shower there than at Graham's, anyway. The girly part of me likes the idea of arriving at dinner all dolled up and ready to knock Graham's socks off, instead of allowing him to peek behind the curtain and realize how many times I poke myself in the eye while getting my eyeliner just right. Plus, I snagged a new dress this afternoon at a boutique I love, and some pretty new lingerie, so I'm all set for date night.

I text Graham that I'll meet him at eight. He texts back that he can't wait to see me—sending another wave of anticipation rushing through my chest—and I burn up the next two hours with a bike ride, a shower, and a blow-out at the salon on the corner.

At seven fifty, I slip through the thick dinner crowd at Eataly on Fifth Avenue, the combination authentic Italian grocery and vast palace of sinfully delicious eateries of my dreams. But my favorite, of course, is the rooftop bar and grill. I make my way to the hostess stand by the elevators, where a big-eyed Italian girl in a red dress informs me Graham is already waiting for me on the roof.

As the elevator zips skyward, I realize Graham never actually said we were meeting at Birreria, and I smile. There's something special about not needing any other directions aside from *your favorite restaurant at eight.*

He knows me.

And I know him.

As I exit the elevator, I head directly for the far end of the bar, where I suspect Graham will be sitting with a half pint of the on-site brewery's latest concoction. And he is.

"Hey there, Mr. Campbell," I say as I come to a stop beside him.

He turns from the view of the post-sunset pink sky behind the skyscrapers of Manhattan, his eyes lighting up in a way that makes me thankful for showers, blowouts, and smoky ash eyeliner that exactly matches my short-sleeved sweater dress.

"Hello, Miss Murphy." He shakes his head as his gaze skims up and down, taking me in with an appreciation that makes me feel like the most beautiful woman on the rooftop. "You're stunning tonight."

"Thank you," I say, reaching out to smooth his tie. "You don't look bad yourself. I like you in a tie."

"Note to self—skip the gym and keep the tie more often." He drops a ten-dollar bill on the bar and slides off his stool, motioning toward the front of the restaurant. "Let's see if our table's ready. I checked with the hostess a few minutes ago, and she said it should be set soon."

"Perfect. I'm starving," I admit, shivering slightly as he puts his hand at the small of my back, guiding me through the growing crowd milling around the bar. Even through my clothes, his touch is enough to send electricity zipping across my skin.

"Cold?" he asks.

I shake my head, saved from having to say more as the hostess makes eye contact with Graham and motions for us to follow her up the steps to the dining area. I don't know why I'm suddenly feeling so self-conscious, but I'm nearly as nervous as I was that first night at Patio West.

Okay, that's a lie. I know exactly why I'm feeling self-conscious, and I decide to confront the issue head-on.

As soon as we're seated with menus and the hostess has stepped away with assurances that our server will be with us soon, I brace my hands on the table and lean in to whisper, "Thank you for the flowers. And the dessert. I'm sorry we fought."

Graham leans in, mirroring my pose. "We didn't fight. We had conflicting opinions that were amicably resolved with assurances and presents."

"Very nice presents. The flowers were incredible," I continue in a soft voice. "But still. You were right. I was letting the meeting with Lucy affect my thinking when that really has nothing to do with us."

"Exactly. That was a very different situation."

"Totally different," I whisper with a firm nod.

Graham's forehead wrinkles as he whispers back, "Why are we whispering?"

My grin turns into a laugh. "I don't know," I say at normal volume, my shoulders relaxing away from my ears as I sit back in my chair. "Growing up, my dad had a thing about keeping dinner conversation light and as emotion-free as possible. I guess he got in my head a little."

"Parents will do that to you," Graham agrees. "I can't leave the apartment without doing a walk-through to make sure all the lights are off. I keep hearing my dad's voice in my head preaching the evils of wasting electricity."

"Aw, Bob," I say affectionately, thinking of his gruff, no-nonsense father, who loves to laugh—loudly—at anything and everything. "How's he doing? Did they let him back in the fishing club yet?"

"Not yet," Graham says. "But he and Mom took up tennis so he has an outlet for his competitive streak. From what he tells me, they're crushing it in the mixed doubles over-fifty-five division in the local league."

I shake my head in admiration. "That's awesome."

"It is. Now as long as they can resist the urge to play each other too often, they should be able to make it to the over-sixty-five division without filing for divorce. The only thing they love more than each other is winning."

"No. I've seen the way they look at the other. You can't fool me, Campbell. They are proof that love can last."

His smile softens. "Yeah, they are."

I start to ask him if his mom's still working part-time, when our server appears. Graham lifts a brow in my direction as he points to the menu. "The usual, I assume?"

I nod. "Yes, with the chimichurri on the side and—"

"No beans on the antipasto plate," he finishes before communicating the rest of our order. We both love to try new things, but when the flank steak, truffle pasta, and antipasto variety platter are this good, I can't bring myself to part from tradition.

"My mouth is already watering," I confess, biting my lip as our server hurries away. "You're going to have to fight me for the last mozzarella ball tonight."

Graham laughs. "You can have it. I had more than my share last time we were here, before Thanksgiving, when you had to leave early so you wouldn't miss your show. How was that one, by the way? *Funny Farm*, wasn't it?"

"*Fun Home*," I correct with a roll of my eyes. Graham is pretty well versed in the classic musicals, but I haven't dragged his appreciation into the current century just yet. "It was incredible. Beautiful. Funny. Heart-wrenching. I ugly-cried so hard at the end I had to go to the ladies' room as soon as the curtain was up and clean the mascara off my cheeks."

His brows draw together in concern. "And that was an enjoyable night at the theater for you?"

I nod enthusiastically. "Oh, yes. It was. The story is about a lot of things, but the theme that got to me was how the fear and shame we don't deal with as we grow up is passed on to our children. A kind of legacy of pain, you know? And how loving and accepting yourself, even when society is telling you that you don't deserve love, truly is a gift you give the world, not just the person in the mirror. I thought that was beautiful. And important."

"Wow," Graham says, sobering. "I didn't realize musicals got that heavy."

I shrug. "Sometimes. There were funny parts, too, but I think that was the part I needed to hear."

Graham's head tilts quizzically. "Really? But you always seem so . . . you. Unapologetically you, and happy about it."

I grin. "Well, I am usually. But there are times, like when facing down my twenty-sixth birthday without experiencing things I was certain I would have experienced by this point, that I struggle."

He nods thoughtfully, holding my gaze as a slow smile curves his lips.

"What?" I laugh again. "Why are you smiling?"

"I'm smiling because I'm glad you decided to stop waiting for experiences to find you and decided to hunt them down for yourself. And I'm glad I'm the one who gets to show you what you've been missing."

My cheeks flush, and my chest feels warmer than it did before. "Me, too."

His eyes glittering, he adds, "And you are absolutely worthy of love and acceptance. You're one of my favorite people and, as you know, I have excellent taste."

My gaze falls to my bread plate as the warm feeling floods through the rest of me, all the way to the tips of my fingertips and toes. And I know what this feeling is. It is familiar to me from bear hugs from my brother, and hour-long girl-talk sessions with Chloe, and long, lazy summers with my grandmother before she passed away, learning how to knit and laughing over old episodes of *SNL*.

But I've never experienced it like this, all tangled up with wanting to press my lips to every inch of the person who's inspiring the sensation, to thank him for making me feel loved in my body as well as in my soul.

I know Graham doesn't love me romantically. But his words are the perfect reminder of why this is so right . . . and so dangerous.

Who better to teach me how to make love than someone who loves me already?

But who is it riskier to learn with than someone I know I could fall so hard for, who only loves me as a friend?

"You okay, Butterfly?" he asks, his hand coming to rest on my knee under the table.

I look up, forcing a smile. "Yes, I am." I take a deep breath and add in a teasing tone, "Though I'm not going to look very sexy in whatever lingerie you have picked out for our lesson later. I can't resist seconds of the truffle stuff, and I'm not even going to try."

"You will always be sexy in anything you wear," he says, giving my knee a gentle squeeze. "But I didn't pick out any lingerie for tonight. You want to know why?"

I nod.

He runs his hand up my knee. "Because the lesson I want you to learn is that you're beautiful just as you are. You're gorgeous in whatever you choose for yourself, be that panties, T-shirts, music, friends, work, or anything else."

A flush spreads over my chest as my heart beats

harder, faster, trying desperately to wiggle closer to him. "Thank you," I say, because it's all I can manage.

"Besides, the other lesson for tonight is that sex can be amazing when you do whatever feels right for you. When you're ready, whenever that is."

When I'm ready . . .

I nod, nerves and breathless excitement flaring behind my ribs, making it feel like a balloon is inflating in my chest. But before I can give verbal confirmation that yes, I'm ready, all ready, *so* ready, the server arrives with food and share plates. So much food. Delicious, incredible food.

But I can barely taste it.

I can't focus on the rich, yet delicate cream sauce or the perfectly firm pillows of smoky mozzarella. I am only partially present for my conversation with Graham about Luna, his best friend from grad school who is preparing to launch a new fleet of food trucks in the financial district, or our discussion of why Birreria's tiramisu is superior to all others in the city.

All I can think about is that tonight is the night. In an hour, maybe less, I will know things that I've never known, and I will never be the same. And Graham will be there, and he will forever be a part of this story, this decision, this transition from one stage of my life to the next.

And yes, it's a little scary. But it's also right. Because I'm ready.

andle with care.

That's what I keep telling myself during the car ride to my place.

Be gentle.

Take it slow.

But when she kisses me like this, all lips, teeth, and a newly discovered confidence that's downright addictive, I don't want to take it slow. I want to slam my lips to hers, tangle my hands in her silky hair, yank her head back, and leave a trail of rough kisses up the gorgeous column of her throat.

I try to slow my pace, but she's leading now, kissing me hard and relentlessly, almost as if she's saying over and over *I'm ready, I'm ready, I'm ready.*

She might be, but I need a breather for a second.

I press my hands on her shoulders and separate us. "CJ, you're driving me crazy."

She nibbles on the corner of her lips. "Isn't that the goal?"

155

"Butterfly, you've already reached the goal. We need to slow down till we get to my place. I don't want to hurt you, and right now, you're kind of making me want to pull you under me and take you right here in the car."

Mischief sparkles in her eyes. "I thought you were the one who said you won't break?"

I let out a shaky laugh. "Yes, I remember. But it's *you* I'm concerned about."

"News flash," she whispers. "I'm not going to break, either. And I really like wild, crazy kissing."

I close my eyes and groan, my bones humming with pleasure. I glance out the window, grateful for the familiar view of the buildings on my street. The car pulls to the curb, and I thank Gary.

A few minutes later, the elevator doors close, and I press CJ to the wall, returning the favor from the car, kissing her neck, sucking on her jaw, and devouring her lips. This time, she's the one who groans first.

"Payback," I tease.

"I want more payback," she says in a dirty whisper.

I oblige with more ravenous kisses.

She moans my name, and it sounds needy and desperate, and that's exactly how I want her tonight. Because if she feels that way, then there's a damn good chance I can make her first time amazing for her.

That's how I want it to be.

When the doors open, and we walk down the hall, the words *handle with care* flash again through my mind. But there are new ones, too. *Listen to her.*

She's been telling me something.

She doesn't want to be treated like a box filled with china. She wants me to treat her like the woman she is. And I'm determined to give her exactly what she wants, everything she needs.

Once inside my home, she turns to me and whispers, "Bedroom. Now. Please."

A shudder racks my body, a bolt of lust that nearly overwhelms me with its power. *Her* power. This woman is so goddamn sexy. She might be innocent in body, but in her mind, she knows exactly what she wants.

When we reach my bedroom, I flick the light on low. "I need to see you." My eyes roam over her from head to toe, loving the way she looks in that dress. She kicks off her shoes as I let my fingertips play at the hem. A soft smile is my reward as she lifts her arms, and I pull the sweater fabric over her head.

I groan, probably louder than the last time I came, because of what I see underneath. She kills me with her sexiness, slays me with her pure sensuality.

Tonight, she's wearing white. A lace demi-cup bra and lace panties. They are so simple and so pretty, and so intoxicatingly her. The color is a secret message, just for me. She's giving me this gift of herself, and she's wrapped her gorgeous body up so perfectly.

"See? I didn't need to send you anything. You knew exactly what you needed to wear to feel beautiful." I run the back of my fingers over her cheek. "Do you feel beautiful? Because you are. So beautiful." I press my body against hers, letting her feel the evidence of how much I want her.

"Yes. I do." A ragged breath falls from her lips as my

hands move to her breasts. I cover them, kneading them, squeezing them, then my hands band around her back, and I unhook her bra. Before the soft material can fall to the floor, I grab it and toss it on the bureau.

I bury my face between her perfect tits, licking the tops, sucking on her nipples. I walk her backward to the bed and lay her down on it. She grabs a pillow, sets it under her head, and looks at me with wide eyes.

"There's only one rule tonight," I say as I unknot my tie and take it off. "You tell me if something doesn't feel right. Be open with me. I need to know how you feel so I can make it good for you. Can you do that?"

She nods.

I bite my lip as I slide her white panties down. "Wait. There's one more rule."

She raises an eyebrow.

"I need to eat you first."

A naughty smile is my reward. "If you insist."

After I tug her panties off, I bury my face between her legs, licking and kissing her glorious wetness, and driving her wild in seconds. Soon enough, she's rocking into my mouth, grabbing my hair, pulling me even closer. Her moans intensify, carrying across the night. Soon, she's nearing the edge, and I kiss her hungrily, greedily, until I can taste her flooding my tongue, covering my lips.

"So good," she moans as she drifts back to earth. "So, so good."

"My pleasure. Every second." I stand, unbuttoning my shirt as she blinks open her eyes. They are glassy and sex-hazy, and her hair is a wild mess.

"I think you're trying to get me drunk on orgasms," she breathes.

"I see absolutely no reason why you shouldn't come as often as possible." Tossing my shirt to the floor, I move my hands to my jeans. She shakes her head and sits up, reaching for the button. "Let me."

I drop my hands to my sides and stare as she unzips my jeans, pushing them down my thighs, allowing my dick to make its appearance. A soft, sexy sigh falls from her gorgeous mouth.

As I take off the rest of my clothes, she gazes up at me, excitement and anticipation clear in her beautiful brown eyes. She's so eager, so curious, and it's such a gift to have her trust, to be the first person to experience her like this.

My heart beats faster, from pleasure but also from something more, something entirely new that I'm only beginning to understand. But I can't sort it out now. All I can think about is how much I need to be closer to her, joined with her, feeling her tight around me for the first time.

I grab a condom from my wallet.

As I open it, she grabs my wrist and says, "There's something I need to say."

I wince inside, but steel myself for whatever comes next. I'm dying to be inside her, but I don't want her to do anything she isn't ready for. And as I look in her eyes, it hits me—I care so much more for her than I realized before our classes started. And this has become so much more than lessons in seduction.

If she's not ready, I'll wait, blue balls be damned. If

she needs another month, hell, a year, I'll be here. I'll wait until she's ready.

I just want it to be me that she's ready for.

"What is it, Butterfly? Tell me anything," I say gently.

Her gaze locks with mine. "I'm so glad it's you."

And if I wasn't already lost for her, that pretty much seals the deal.

CHAPTER 20

CJ

*J*ust because I've carried my V card for a quarter of a century doesn't mean I've kept a pure mind, too.

Quite the contrary.

My brain has run wild. My imagination has frolicked in Naughtyville thousands of times, and though the details—the catalyst and the location—varied, one aspect was nearly always the same.

Graham.

Him over me, him inside me, him being my first.

That's what I've wanted most of all.

A rush of anticipation fills my body as he climbs over me, but then anxiety rises up, pulling at me, tightening in my belly. A thousand thoughts race through my mind, and my heart jams in my throat, but as I look up at his handsome face, I know it isn't having sex for the first time that's making me nervous.

What scares me is that I'm already failing at the lesson I tried to teach myself this afternoon.

My heart isn't in another room.

I'm here, all in, heart, body, and mind.

It's wildly exciting and completely terrifying. But how can I even consider turning back when this is everything I've dreamt of and so much more?

I reach my arms around his neck, pull him even closer, and press my lips to his, kissing away my fears. "I'm *so* ready," I whisper.

"I like the *so*." He positions himself, rubs the head of his erection against me, and I gasp. A pulse beats between my legs, where I'm wet, ridiculously wet.

Relax. I spread my legs wider, letting my knees fall open, inviting him in.

He pushes the tip inside. "Okay?" he pants.

A warm, tingly feeling spreads through me. "More than okay."

I draw a sharp breath as he sinks deeper inside. Deeper, deeper, maybe halfway in, and holy hell.

He's stretching me, and for a moment I feel as if I'm being ripped apart. I grit my teeth, my muscles tensing against the sting.

"Butterfly." His voice is laced with worry

I try to will away the pain, but damn, it hurts. "I'm fine," I mutter.

"You're not fine. Talk to me."

I remember I promised I would be honest. I loop my arms tighter around his neck, needing to hold him close as I confess, "It hurts, Graham. But I don't want to stop. So please don't."

He sighs heavily, but doesn't move. I look up at him, seeing concern, care, and so much more in his eyes. I see him here with me, in every way, and suddenly I can breathe. And that changes the game.

As I pull in another breath, I start to relax.

"Perfect," he whispers. "Just breathe, baby. Take all the time you need."

Another breath, and the stinging sensation fades a little more.

Slowly, the hurt subsides, giving way to another rush of warmth and desire, the need to get even closer to this man who is so sweetly patient with me.

I wrap my legs around him. "Now. I want you inside me. All the way."

There's something about saying those words that empowers me. That emboldens my body to accept everything he has to give. This is my choice, my man, my moment. I give myself over to all the possibilities, all the hunger, all the emotion filling my chest to overflowing.

I swallow hard and grab his ass, pulling him deeper.

He slides another inch, and like the soft, final notes of a song, the pain ends.

Another song begins, a primal melody that is beautiful, natural, and oh-so right.

I still feel stretched, full, but I also feel something wholly new. A spark spreads up my chest to my arms, down to my fingers. This sensation is warm, it's floaty—it's what I've always wanted.

A smile spreads across my face.

Graham laughs lightly. "Looks like everything is okay?"

"So much better than okay," I say, and I can't stop smiling. "It's like champagne. You don't know what to make of it the first time you taste it, and then you just want more."

"You want more, baby?"

"Oh yes . . ." I start to move with him, my hips rocking up, sensations building and rising inside me.

His hips swivel, and he goes deeper. But never too hard or too rough. Always with just the right amount of pressure, just the right amount of *him in me.*

God, a man is inside me—*Graham* is inside me—and it is every bit as incredible as I ever imagined.

My body grows hotter, my skin damper. My heart jackhammers as he moves and I move with him, and somehow, we find the most wonderful rhythm.

Together.

Gently but firmly, he guides my leg higher on his hip, opening me more as he thrusts into me. I'm trembling all over as a full, heavy feeling ripples through me. I'm being wickedly, deliciously turned inside out.

And then, he slides his hand down between us, touching me where I want him most, and that sends me soaring. He rubs and strokes, and soon I'm mindless with pleasure. I'm lost in all these new sensations as he fills me and zeroes in on where everything feels like bliss.

Soon, that's all I feel. I've passed the brink. I'm reaching something inevitable. Something that was always meant to happen this way, just exactly this way.

There's a flash of ecstatic oblivion as desire curls inward, tightens, and then I let go, I fall, and the waves of pleasure overcome me. I reach the edge as he fills me, as he makes love to me, as he takes me over the cliff.

A few seconds later, he's there with me, too. Saying

my name. Saying how good it feels. Telling me he's coming.

I'm drowning in the sweetest heat as I watch him thrust one last time then come apart, shuddering, his jaw clenched as he moans low in his throat. And this is another wondrous first for me, watching a man climax inside me, and I like this part just as much as I like my own orgasms.

Probably because I'm falling in love with him.

That's the part that's truly going to hurt.

Because in a few more nights, this will end.

CHAPTER 21

GRAHAM

*a*ll day Friday at the office, all I can think about is CJ. Making love to CJ. How sweet and sexy and incredible she was last night, and how much I need to have her naked in my arms again, calling my name while she comes on my cock, ASA-fucking-P.

We're more than halfway through our seven days, and there's still so much ground left to cover, so many lessons left to learn . . .

The afternoon is a full course in patience, as CJ and I exchange mutually frustrated text messages about how intolerable it is to have to remain clothed and in separate offices in different parts of the city all day.

The evening is a master class in anticipation as I treat CJ to happy hour martinis and my fingers skimming up the inside of her thigh beneath the tablecloth at our corner booth.

Friday night begins with a lesson in how much fun we can have in the shower together, with nothing but body wash and a fresh sponge. It ends with a four-hour tutorial in going nearly all night long.

Never has exhaustion been so sweet.

Saturday morning dawns with a warm yellow glow through the curtains that has me up and at 'em, even though I closed my eyes less than five hours ago.

But I'm full of energy. I finally have an entire day stretching out in front of me with nothing but CJ in it. No work. No meetings. Just full-immersion sex education for the next forty-eight hours. I kiss her softly on her forehead, slide quietly out of bed, and head down the hall to the kitchen with a spring in my step.

I whistle as I start the coffeepot and dig deep in the drawers for the pans I rarely use. Sure, there's a voice in my head warning that there's no reason to be so excited —this sex fling is going to be over tomorrow night and there will be no more lessons, no more CJ in my bed, no more waking up with her warm and delicious in my arms—but I ignore that voice.

No buzz-killing on the menu today. Just buzz-encouraging.

Which means pancakes and extra-dark French roast coffee.

Now if I can just find that pan . . .

The one you use to, um, cook things . . .

CHAPTER 22

CJ

I wake up feeling like I barely survived one of the hard-core boot-camp weekends Chloe drags me to every June before bathing suit season.

I'm sore in every single one of my muscles, even ones I wasn't aware existed until they started aching. My brain is a sluggish lump sitting heavily in my skull, refusing to think thoughts more eloquent than "Coffee now. Coffee good," and I'm so exhausted I'm pretty sure I'm going to need assistance to drag my butt out of this heavenly soft bed.

Oh yeah . . . and I'm also completely giddy.

Graham is mine for the weekend, and I refuse to let anything get in the way of my last two days with him. Two days of Graham making me feel earth-shattering, mind-blowing, perspective-revolutionizing things that have made it abundantly clear what the fuss is all about. The fuss is about orgasms and more orgasms and yet even more orgasms delivered by a sexy-as-hell man who tells me that I'm the most beautiful thing he's ever seen, the sweetest thing he's ever tasted.

I sigh as my mouth begins to water. I'm not sure if it's memories of Graham, or the scent of vanilla and sugar in the air, but I'm suddenly starving.

After a full-body stretch, I swing my feet to the floor and pull on one of Graham's T-shirts and a pair of panties.

I find him in the kitchen, wearing nothing but boxer briefs and a chef's apron. Only Graham could mix adorable and sexy so well.

A skillet sizzles on the stove. Oblivious to my presence, he hustles about the kitchen, pulling items from the refrigerator, setting them on the counter, and rushing back to the stove where the sweet smell is coming from.

Pancakes?

I sneak quietly up behind him to plant my elbows on the center island. "Well, well. I didn't know you cooked."

Graham spins with a slightly harried smile. "Good morning, Butterfly. How did you sleep?"

"Like the dead," I confess. "But in a good way."

He grins. "Me, too. And yes, I like to use the kitchen once a year or so, so it doesn't feel neglected."

"Biannually, eh?" I shake my head as I tease, "I'm thinking that doesn't bode well for the quality of these pancakes."

He places the bowl of batter on the counter and snatches his spatula from near the sink, where several other bowls of lumpy batter have apparently already been discarded. "You wound me, Murphy. Here I am, slaving over a hot stove to feed your sexy body pancakes and—"

"Graham, I think—"

"And you're insulting my cooking prowess before you've even—"

"Graham," I say more urgently as smoke begins to rise behind him.

"—tasted the fruits of my labor or—"

"Graham, the stove," I break in, jabbing a finger at the skillet, where tendrils of brown smoke are quickly turning black. "Your pancakes are burning."

Graham whirls around. "Shit." He snatches the entire pan—charred mess and all—from the stove and practically tosses it into the sink before turning on the water, sending the smell of soggy, burning batter whooshing through the kitchen.

"Exhaust!" I hurry around the island and flip the exhaust switch. Immediately, the cloud of smoke begins to clear.

I turn to Graham, who is looking positively sheepish with his spatula in one hand and a potholder in the other, and I burst out laughing. "Give me that." I take his spatula and use it to make shooing motions. "Make way for a professional. You clearly need a proper class in when to flip your pancake."

His brows bob playfully up and down. "That sounds dirty. I didn't know you wanted to flip my pancake."

"Oh, but I do," I say in my best sexy voice, tossing my hair over my shoulder as I grab the least offensive bowl of batter from the counter. "Get me a fresh skillet, baby. The student is about to become the teacher."

Graham offers a snappy salute. "Yes, ma'am. One fresh skillet coming up."

Ten minutes later, I've instructed my eager pupil in the proper temperature, timing, and flipping technique to achieve perfectly browned pancakes every time. And I actually manage to get a small stack of ready-to-eat hotcakes stacked on a plate next to the stove before Graham circles his arms around me, and my devotion to the curriculum begins to wander.

"You are so hot right now." His fingers slip beneath my T-shirt to skim my ribs as he kisses my neck. "All bossy, taking charge of my kitchen . . ."

"Someone had to take you in hand." I bite my lip as his palms glide higher. "You're clearly a pancake-flipping virgin."

"You're so right." He cups my breasts, making my next breath rush in on a gasp of awareness as his thumb brushes across my nipple. "And so generous and patient with me. I wonder how I can ever repay you."

Flipping off the heat to the burner, I lean against him, offering him unimpeded access, glancing over my shoulder to meet his gaze as I whisper, "I have a few ideas about repayment."

"Oh, yeah?" He somehow manages to maintain his innocent expression even as he rolls my nipples harder, making me fight to hold in a moan. "Might they have anything to do with a lesson in up-against-the-refrigerator sex?"

I lick my lips, pressing them tight together as hunger floods my every cell. "I think refrigerator sex is a good start. Though, I may require further payment after breakfast. I have some questions about alternative uses for maple syrup that I would like to explore."

Graham makes a contemplative sound deep in his throat. "Tell me more."

But before I can answer, and tell him exactly what I have in mind for syrup, he's captured my mouth with his, sending the taste of sweet, sugary coffee and Graham flooding through my mouth.

And it is as fantastic as always.

The best taste. My favorite taste.

Pancakes are definitely going to have to wait.

CHAPTER 23

CJ

*T*he lesson in alternative uses for syrup goes well—*very* well, if I do say so myself. By the time I'm finished with Graham, he's so useless I have to bring his plate of pancakes to him on the kitchen floor and feed him syrup-soaked pieces until he recovers his strength.

"You're such a drama king," I tease as I pop a bite between his lips before stabbing another triangle for myself.

He smiles, his eyes closed as he chews. "Am not. This is what happens to a man when you give him the best blow job of his life." He continues before I can challenge the truth of that statement. "Besides, I'm conserving my energy for the afternoon's adventures."

"Oh, yeah?" I ask, intrigued. "And what might those be?"

His eyes open in a sleepy, sexy way that makes my body start to hum again. "You'll see. It's a surprise.

LAUREN BLAKELY & LILI VALENTE

Something to push us both out of our comfort zones. It's going to be fun."

I arch an eyebrow, unsure what he's getting at. "If you say so."

"But you will need to dress for moderate to strenuous physical activity in the out of doors."

My brows lift. "You want to go outside?"

"Hard to conduct the lesson I have in mind in an apartment."

I twist my features into an exaggerated frown. "All right. If you insist. But I confess I was having fantasies about keeping you in bed all day. With few to no clothes on."

"Tempting. Very tempting, but there will be time for that tomorrow. Today, we're taking it to the streets. Get dressed, Butterfly. We're going out."

An hour later, after two subway rides—a trip to The Village Vet to check on Stephen King and spoil him with petting and tuna treats, and a walk through a part of Brooklyn I haven't seen before—we arrive at the Prospect Park outdoor roller-skating rink, and Graham holds open the gate to usher me inside.

"You have to be kidding," I say, my gaze sliding to the families, couples, and wild, sticky-faced kids rolling in frenzied circles. "We both stink at roller-skating."

"Which is why this is a perfect chance to learn something new together."

"While I love the idea, might I remind you of the debacle known as Chloe's roller-disco party two years ago?"

"I know. That's what'll make it fun. We'll fall on our assess in unity."

I shoot him a skeptical stare. "Have you forgotten that you nearly wound up with a shattered tailbone? I, for one, have a crystal-clear visual of you landing smack on your cute butt in the middle of the rink."

He smirks. "You think my ass is cute."

I roll my eyes. "Obviously. But that's neither here nor there. Why don't you park that cute butt on a paddleboat and we can do that together instead? They rent those. I saw a sign back there."

He shakes his head, wiggling his eyebrows. "I'd rather see your cute butt skating in front of me."

I laugh at him and then take a deep breath. Come to think of it, what if I do fall on my butt? What if he falls on his?

We'll get back up. We'll keep on skating. We'll figure it out together.

A fresh surge of confidence zips through me. "Fine, then let's lace up, speedy. I'm ready to race if you are," I say with a wink.

"Oh, I was born ready." He takes my hand. "And don't worry, I won't let you fall."

His words echo as we head to the rental counter.

I won't let you fall . . .

Oh, but Graham, it's already too late, don't you see? I'm already falling. Falling so fast and I can't seem to stop.

But I don't say any of those things out loud. I just grip his hand, determined to hold tight for the time we have left.

* * *

WE AREN'T DISCO kings on roller skates. I'm not

bopping along like a roller-derby girl, and he's not a skate god on wheels. We are stiff and silly-looking and laughing more than any other couple on the rink.

And I like it that way.

As I watch him glide unsteadily around the turns, a little clunky at first but a whole lot determined, I find I'm even more attracted to him than I was before we arrived. I love that he's not amazing at skating. I love that he's awkward, but he's doing it anyway. He's not letting imperfection get in the way of a good time.

And neither am I.

I make it around a few times, skating more comfortably with each lap. Then he skates a few feet in front of me and comes to an only semi-shaky stop.

"Impressive," I observe.

He holds out a hand. "How about a spin?"

I laugh, shaking my head. "No way. Straight ahead without falling is enough excitement for me."

"One spin," his wheedles, fingers curling around mine. "C'mon. No risk, no reward."

"I'll fall."

"You won't fall." He takes both my hands, skating slowly in a curve. "I've got you, Butterfly. Trust me."

"I do trust you. Obviously," I say. My heart jerks as his eyes meet mine and something passes between us, something intimate that makes me forget I can't spin in skates.

And in that moment, I'm sure he can see right through me, straight to that starry-eyed dreamer who wants so much more from him than seven days. Will she scare him away?

But he just holds on tight and says, "Look at us. We rock."

We glide faster, spinning in smooth circles, both of us relaxing as we gain confidence. We aren't going to sign up for synchronized skating any time soon, but I'm smiling, and he's grinning, and skating is even more fun with him by my side.

So are sleepovers.

And dinners.

And kitty scavenger hunts.

And pancake-making.

New things are better with him, too.

Like a certain physical activity he's introduced me to. One that's brought me so much closer to him than I ever bargained for.

Love . . . I've fallen in love.

But if I tell him I earned an F in keeping my heart out of this deal, I know there's a good chance I'll lose him as a friend. Graham has firm boundaries, and I've never seen him let a woman as close as I want to be to him.

So close. All the way close.

And I can't risk that. I care about him too much to excise him from my life by pushing for more than he's willing to give.

My chest hurts, and a lump forms in my throat. The lump threatens to turn into something more intense, but I swallow it down.

I'm keeping my chin up and my head in the beautiful now, not the uncertain future. When I look back on this magical week, at least I'll know I soaked it all in, from the first kiss, to hand-holding at the skating rink, to the moment we say goodbye.

Too bad there's no class that can prepare me to let him go. Of that, I'm sure.

CHAPTER 24

GRAHAM

*T*he day is passing too fast. Way too fucking fast.

I want to slow time. Or pull a *Groundhog Day*, wake up tomorrow, and live this day all over again, just like Bill Murray in the movie, but without the existential angst.

The more I get of CJ without the "just friends" wall that used to stand between us, the more I want of her. She's like mint chocolate chip ice cream. I could eat a gallon of her without stopping.

A part of me wants to tell her that as we stroll across the Brooklyn Bridge. I want to tell her that her smile makes me hopeful in a way I've never been hopeful before, and that having her hand in mine makes me feel like the luckiest bastard on this bridge.

But you don't say those things to a friend you're teaching how to screw.

CJ didn't come to me with a seven-day plan for me to get seven kinds of attached to her. And if I tell her that's happened, I'll risk messing up our friendship forever. She made it clear that this was a sex deal, and I can't let the pancake haze or the skating mojo trick me into thinking she wants more, too.

I want this woman in my life, and I won't take a chance at losing her. Some of her is better than none. I don't want to let her go tomorrow, but I suppose I have to.

CJ sighs happily, looking at the endless sky above us. "This day is perfect. This sky is perfect. It's so beautiful, isn't it? Like a painting."

"Yes, this is a perfect day. Every hour. Every minute." I squeeze her hand as we cross the Brooklyn Bridge into Manhattan, ambling along beside tourists posing for selfies in front of the skyline.

My eyes catch CJ's, and a slow, wicked smile curves her lips. "What are you thinking?" she asks.

My shoulders tense as answers rattle through my brain.

You.

More.

Let's keep doing this.

I'm falling for you.

I part my lips, tempted to throw caution to the wind and blurt out any or all of the above. Tell her that I need her to enroll for another semester of lessons because I'm not anywhere close to ready to let her go.

But I've never said those words before, so I fall back on old habits, waving a dismissive hand. "Just thinking about Monday."

She nods knowingly. "Ah, the board meeting. Of course."

But that's not why I'm thinking of Monday at all.

* * *

WE'RE QUIETER as we finish our walk, and the air cools off rapidly. By the time we make it back into Manhattan, the sun is sinking behind the horizon, leaving a bitter wind in its wake. I call a car service—Gary isn't working this weekend—and CJ and I wait inside a coffee shop till a black town car pulls up five minutes later.

Once inside, I say hello to the driver then raise the partition, taking CJ's hands in mine to warm them up. I rub my palms against hers.

When she lifts her face and meets my eyes, my heart beats faster.

"Hey, you," she says softly. "I had so much fun today."

"Me, too. The best time."

"I'll miss this," she whispers, and with those words something inside my chest cracks. It's out of nowhere, but not unexpected.

It's been happening all week long. Since she approached me at brunch. Since the night at the St. Regis. Since she settled into my home.

But it was simmering beneath the surface well before that. When I look back on the last two years, this woman has been here, right beside me, every step of the way. She's seen me at the toughest times and the greatest times.

We've endured loss together, and now, somehow, we've found ourselves on the other side of grief and in each other's arms.

And when I look into her eyes, that's where I want to be. With her.

I drop my forehead to hers and whisper her name. It's all I can say. I don't know how to give voice to anything more than this. I never have. I've never felt this. I've never fallen so hard, so fast, and so truly for a woman.

All I know is how to touch her, so I use a language I'm fluent in, pressing my lips gently to hers in a tender kiss that I hope tells her what I can't speak aloud. She has to feel it, too, has to know that what's happening between us is worth investing so much more than seven days.

I move my hands under her shirt then down her yoga pants, peeling them off. "I want to watch you ride me in the car."

A wicked grin spreads on her face. "Is this a lesson in seduction?"

I shake my head adamantly. "No. It's not a lesson. It's what I want. It's *all* I want. You're all I want."

"You're all I want, too."

I push down my jeans, find a condom in my wallet, and roll it down my length as the car weaves through Saturday evening traffic.

Nervousness flashes in her eyes as she glances at the window.

"No one can see us," I reassure her.

She nods then holds my face. "And I don't care if they do."

My heart thumps hard. She's become so daring. Or maybe she was all along. Maybe she just needed someone to turn the key, to unlock her. God, how I want to be the only one who has that key.

But I will savor every second of her right now as I bring her down on me.

A sharp intake of breath.

Her wetness.

Her arms around my neck.

Her lips on my jaw.

My hands on her body.

Her taste on my tongue.

She moves on me, and I push up into her, and we engage in a time-honored Manhattan tradition—getting it on in the back of a town car.

Only it hardly feels like getting it on.

It feels like coming together.

Like making love.

Like being as close as I can be to the woman who's opened my heart.

That's what she's done. She's taught me something so much more vital than what I've shown her.

She's taught me how it feels to fall in love.

CHAPTER 25

CJ

*A*fter the past week, I thought I knew what making love felt like. But just now in the car, with Graham's breath in my lungs and his heart beating in sync with mine and every kiss feeling like a confession that he feels the way I feel . . .

I've never been so close.

So deep.

So completely in harmony with another person.

I know he feels it, too.

At least, I strongly suspect that he does.

I suspect it enough to climb up onto the high dive, wiggle my fingers in the rare air up here, where the wind is wild and full of possibilities, and seriously consider taking a leap into the great unknown.

As soon as Graham closes the door behind us and flips on the lights in his apartment, moving into the kitchen to fetch the mountain of take-out menus from the drawer, I draw a deep breath, turn my courage up to maximum strength, and say, "You know, I've been thinking a lot about my parents."

He looks up from rifling through the menus, his brows raised. "Yeah? Why's that?"

"Well, my mom died when I was so young, I don't remember what her relationship with my dad was like." I keep my tone casual as I wander to the island, crossing my arms on top. "And then Dad married Betty, and that's a total circus. I mean, I know they care about each other, but he literally does anything my stepmother tells him to do. It's like he got a lobotomy along with that wedding ring."

Graham snorts. "Well, Betty is a pretty hot number. Better men than your dad have been sucked into a siren's sex vibe."

"Gross." I make a gagging sound, and Graham laughs.

"Old people do it, too, baby. Or so I hear, when my mom has a few too many hot toddies on Christmas Eve and overshares about her last ski trip with the old man." He holds up two brightly colored menus. "Thai food from the spicy curry place, or the place with the killer summer rolls?"

"But that's why I love your parents," I say, determined not to be swept off course by food, no matter how starved I am. "They still love each other so much, even after all the years and everything they've been through. It makes me want to believe that love can last, even though I haven't seen it up close in my own life." I swallow, my tongue sweeping out to dampen my dry lips as I inch closer to the edge of that diving board, my

185

heart hammering against my ribs. "What about you? Do you think romance can last forever?"

He pauses, shaking his head as he glances down into the drawer. "I don't know, Butterfly. I've never felt anything like that before."

I freeze. I can't move. Can't speak. I don't even want to think. I want to rewind this moment and change the script, make different words emerge from his mouth.

But I can't. The truth is out and there's no going back.

I've never felt anything like that before.

As cold, harsh reality hits, I'm suddenly tumbling, falling . . . but not down into the sparkling water. I'm stumbling backward off the wrong end of the diving board, plummeting toward the concrete on a collision course that's going to leave me battered and bruised.

He's never felt anything like that before.

Which means he doesn't feel it for me.

This is one-sided. This is me, the wide-eyed virgin, falling for the first guy she slept with. My chest heaves, and a stupid hitch tries to work its way up my throat. But I won't let on that I'm every bit as much of a fool as I've feared.

Taking a deep breath, I square my shoulders and fight like hell to maintain a calm facade. If I stay strong, I can try to preserve our friendship, our working relationship. That's what matters now.

Don't let on, CJ.

He clears his throat, and when he looks up again, he's smiling and holding a dark menu with sushi on the front. "How about sushi? Keep dinner classic and elegant after a day of adventure?"

I stare at him, amazed that this is so simple for him, astonished that his stomach is his top priority when the floor is slipping from under me.

But his focus on food is further proof that I'm in this alone.

And I need to extricate myself from this situation the same damn way.

My lips part to say sushi is fine, but I can't seem to make the words come out. I'm too mortified. Too sad. Too deep in grief for what's never going to be.

But thankfully, Graham's cell buzzes at that exact moment, sparing me from saying sushi is fine for heartbreak, thank you very much—my one piece of good luck this evening.

He picks it up and is silent for a moment.

"Whoa, slow down, Brian." Graham paces out of the kitchen into the dining area overlooking the Hudson. "Is she okay? Are you okay?" He nods, pacing faster. "Got it. No worries. You go have a baby. I'll take care of everything else." More nodding, and now a hand raked through his hair. "Absolutely. And let us know how it goes. We're all rooting for you guys and a safe, easy birth."

Graham ends the call and turns back to me with a huff of breath. "Babies." He laughs once. "They don't come on a schedule, do they?"

My brow pinches. Am I supposed to answer that? But I don't need to because he keeps going. "I have to head into the office. Brian was putting the finishing touches on our new ads tonight so our ad agency can finalize the package for the board by Monday afternoon. But his wife—"

"Is having a baby." I force a smile, pretending I'm not in the middle of an emotional meltdown. "I heard. You go take care of business. I'll be fine."

"Are you sure? I don't want to leave you here starving to death."

"I can order food. I'm a big girl." I make shooing motions with both hands, pathetically thrilled that I haven't broken down in front of him. "Now go on, get everything handled. I'll be fine."

And I am fine.

Or I will be. I even manage to kiss him goodbye without falling to pieces and crying like an idiot virgin who had no idea how easy it would be to let love become inextricably bound up with pleasure.

But once Graham is gone and I'm alone in his house, with his leather-bound books chosen by an interior decorator, and the pans he never uses, and the sterile decorations in the bedroom that make it clear all this man does here is sleep, the truth settles on my chest, crushing in its weight.

Graham is married to his work.

Work is his steady date, his primary focus, and the drumbeat that makes his heart dance. Women have always been a passion for him, but never as anything more than entertainment, something fun to appreciate and enjoy in his spare time once the work day is done. He told me so himself at brunch when he said he was on a sex-batical because sex complicates everything. Let alone more than sex…

And I am no different than the women who've come before me.

I. Am. No. Different.

Tears are rising in my eyes when I'm saved by the bell a second time. Though, this bell is a pack of baying wolves – my landlord's ringtone.

"Hello," I sniff as I listen to Arno's heavily accented voice droning on the other end of the line, telling me that my apartment is all fixed and ready to go. "Really?" I ask, unable to believe such a massive mess was set back in order so quickly. "The sink and the tile and everything?"

"Everything, all done," Arno confirms. "They fix it all first day and just call me now to say they check and grout is dry. All done. Good as new."

Well. It looks like the universe is having at least a little mercy on me.

"That's wonderful." I stand, heading toward the bedroom to pack my bag, my mind already made up. "Thank you so much, Arno. I'll be home tonight."

And then I pack. Because I believe in signs. And all the signs are telling me it's time to get out before I give any more of myself away to a man who isn't interested in what I have to give.

CHAPTER 26

GRAHAM

*A*lmost done.
Another slide.
Another photo.
Another set of ads to review.

As I click on the final proof for the new campaign, I study it carefully, making sure every detail, every word is top-notch. Does it reflect the high-end brand we've crafted?

The new models look fantastic—they are every size, shape, and color, and each woman is beautiful in her own way—but I keep seeing CJ in the corset. CJ wearing it better than anyone's ever worn it.

At least in my eyes.

And that's when I realize what this campaign needs.

She was right.

CJ was damn right.

It's not enough to change the images. The cake tagline is crap. These corsets aren't about food. They're about how they make a woman feel.

With a renewed focus, I tap out a few lines. Then I tweak them. I tighten them, and I send one final change back to the ad agency.

"THIS HOLIDAY SEASON, *feel sexier than you've ever felt before.*"

SIMPLE, but on point. That feels so much better than a slogan about candy or food. Women love gorgeous lingerie because of how it makes them feel. And men can't resist a woman who is confident, passionate, and feeling sexy in her skin.

That's what I need to convey. That's what CJ has always shown me when she's worn Adored.

I call my agency contact, not caring that it's Saturday night. He doesn't, either. Sometimes you have to burn the midnight oil. I give him the change, and he tells me he'll make the adjustment and send proofs back to me shortly.

As I wait for him to reply, I review the slides one more time, then head to the conference room where the meeting will be held on Monday. I flick on the lights. All the chairs are empty, of course. It's late on a Saturday night. But as I wander through the room, I picture Monday morning and the big pitch before the board. Before the shareholders. Making it clear I'm 100 percent committed to delivering on my vision.

God, I love this job, this company. I love what Sean and I built. My eyes stray to the photo of Sean and me at the hockey game, and a faint smile tugs at my lips.

He'd be proud, too. We built something from the ground up, and I continue to run it with integrity, treat our employees well, and deliver a superior experience to our consumers.

My smile fades.

Usually, I get a charge being in here, like a pitcher wandering across the mound before a big game, listening to the quiet of a stadium to get psyched up.

But right now, there's a strange hollowness in this room. Maybe because I'm the only one here.

But maybe for another reason.

Because I don't want to be here at all.

I want to be back at my house with *my* woman.

But she's not mine. Not yet. Maybe not ever.

I was being honest with her. I've never felt anything like what my parents have before. Not until now, with her. But I don't know how to do this—how to risk losing the friend I love to win the woman I love, knowing I can't have them both. Maybe I'm foolish to think I could have more with her. She chose me because I have a reputation for knowing what to do in the bedroom, not because of my stellar track record with relationships.

Because that does not fucking exist.

I return to my desk, but there isn't anything in my inbox from the ad agency, even though the clock is ticking closer to nine.

On impulse, I pull out my cell and text CJ.

GRAHAM: What did you have for dinner, Butterfly? I'm

hoping it was something much more delicious than the yogurt I stole from the staff fridge.

CJ: I actually haven't eaten yet. I was too busy picking up Stephen King and grabbing groceries and cat food. My apartment is ready early so I decided to head home.

WHAT? Head home?

For a second, the words make no sense. When I think of home, I think of *my* home, because with CJ there, it finally feels like a home. Like a place I want to hang out on a Wednesday night and watch movies, or lounge in bed on a Sunday morning with coffee and pancakes.

With her. All of it with her.

And a part of me just can't process that she's taken off like that, without a heads-up.

GRAHAM: You left? You didn't tell me. I didn't think your place would be ready so soon.

CJ: I didn't, either. But hey, miracles happen! It's so nice to be home with the kitty. I think he missed me. He's super cuddly and trying to eat my earring. Isn't that sweet?

NO. That's not fucking sweet. She should be with me.

Her crazy cat should be eating . . . a coaster in my house, a belt loop off my jeans, the top of the toothpaste tube.

Anything.

I rub my hand over the back of my neck, trying to make heads or tails of her departure. I cast about for something to say, something to make it clear I'd rather she be with me.

GRAHAM: That's great, but selfish bastard that I am, I was really enjoying having you with me.

I READ it once more and hit send. I lean back in my chair and wait. That ought to at least start making it clear how I feel. I've never poured my heart out to a woman before, but I don't see how she can fail to get the message from that.

I want more of her.

A few seconds later, a reply arrives, and I tense, hoping it's her saying she's called an Uber to meet me back at my place, to stay this night, then the next, then the next.

CJ: I enjoyed it, too. Of course I did. And I know we were supposed to have seven days of lessons, but it's nearly a week, and after today I feel ready. I've learned all I need to make it on my own. But thank you so much. I'll never forget how wonderful you were. You were everything I wanted in a teacher and more.

A TEACHER? That's all I fucking was to her? A goddamn teacher she'll never forget? I stare at her note. I turn my phone upside down, as if I can shake out the true meaning of her message.

But when I read it once more, those cold words mock me.

I was only her teacher.

I wasn't her lover.

She was clear from the start. She wanted lessons in sex. She didn't sign up for romance.

I'm the only one who made that mistake. I'm the jackass who had this all wrong. I scoff, laughing at myself, but it's not fucking funny. It's *ironic*. And it serves me right. Before her, I'd never been in love. Hell, I've never been in a relationship that lasted longer than a couple of months. Of course I'd fuck it up.

And make the rookie mistake of thinking she'd fallen in love with me, too.

But even though I've royally screwed up when it comes to understanding what love is, I'd like to think I at least know respect.

And I need to respect the woman's wishes. So I say something that's true to my feelings while giving her the distance she seems to want.

GRAHAM: Thank you. The pleasure was truly all mine. I loved every second of being with you.

PAST TENSE. *Loved. Was.*

I hit send and immediately bring my thumbs back to texting position. Because this sucks.

There's a painful ache in my chest. It's no longer empty. It just fucking hurts, and I want to say so much more. I want to tell her that I'm not ready for this to end, that I don't want it to end at all. Ever. I want to promise her that I can make all her dreams come true, and that there's no need to make it on her own.

Or, God forbid, make it with some other guy.

The thought makes me sick. Physically ill. Sour inside. To think of some bastard with his hands on my CJ.

But she's made her position clear. So I simply text—

GRAHAM: I'm here whenever you need me, Butterfly. Anytime. Anywhere.

CJ: Thank you. That means a lot to me, Graham.

SHE MEANS A LOT TO ME. She means more to me than she'll ever know.

I don't know how long I sit silently at my desk, numb and more alone than I've felt since my best friend died, but eventually, my inbox dings.

The ads are here.

The new mock-ups are perfect, so I send my approval and then return to the collection of walls where I will sleep tonight.

It doesn't feel like home. Not without her.

CHAPTER 27

CJ

I'm awoken Sunday morning by Stephen King sitting on my pillow, purring as he chews on my hair.

"No, gross," I murmur, pulling him under the covers with me for a snuggle instead. "No chewing, buddy."

But when he starts gnawing on the sleeve of my flannel pajamas, I don't have the heart to stop him. I don't have the heart to do much of anything except lie here and feel low.

So low.

"I miss him already," I whisper to Stevie, my fingers gliding through his fur. "I don't want to go back to being friends. I can't."

Stephen King meows, and I wish I knew what it meant. Deciding I'm not going to get solid advice from a cat—any cat, but Stevie is an especially lost cause—I call Chloe.

"I'm sad," I whisper, when she finally answers on the fourth ring.

Chloe sighs. "Oh no. It happened? He broke your heart?"

"No. I broke it myself." Tears well in my eyes for the hundredth time since last night. "I knew better than to fall for him, but I did it anyway."

"Oh, babe, I'm sorry." Chloe murmurs something to someone else on the other end of the line. Her man of the moment. Because she is not alone, nor alone with a cat. "Want me to come over with donuts? Or some of that gross green stuff if you're on a health kick?"

I clear my throat. "No. I'm fine. I'll go to the gym, maybe. I don't want to ruin your morning." She starts to object, but before she can sacrifice her romance on the altar of my unrequited heart, I insist, "I'm seriously fine. But I need a coffee date tomorrow morning, okay? Before work? Seven thirty at Dr. Insomnia's Coffee and Tea Emporium."

"I'll be there, babe," she says. "And I'm truly happy to come over today if you change your mind. I'm always here for you."

Always here for you . . .

That was what Graham said . . .

And last night wasn't the first time he said it.

A fragment of memory tugs at my mind. It repeats, urging me to listen.

Only I'm not sure why. But it's loud, and insistent, so I pay attention as it demands I go searching for something that must be found. I thank Chloe, hang up, and roll out of bed before Stephen King can get his teeth on my socks, headed for the closet where I keep all my most treasured things.

CHAPTER 28

GRAHAM

That was the worst night's sleep of my life. And I've slept in a coach seat on a red-eye across the country. Hell, I've hit the sack on the floor of my office for an hour of shut-eye after working all night.

But this tossing and turning sucks.

She's not next to me when I wake, and that feels like an affront to the fabric of the universe. When I wander into the kitchen to make a cup of coffee, the sink reminds me of her.

The motherfucking sink.

The stove holds a memory, for Christ's sake.

Good thing I don't use it, or I'd think of her every time I cooked, and now I've found yet another reason to never make a meal I can't take out or order in.

I heave a sigh, trudge back down the hall, and curse my bed once more for taunting me with images of her on it, in it, curled up with me.

Hell, it's been less than twelve hours, and everything

is a reminder of the woman I fell unexpectedly ass over elbow for.

It's a cruel joke. Is this what a broken heart feels like? How does anyone endure this? Get through it? All I know to do when my mind is a traffic pileup is to run. Maybe it will work with a piled-up heart, too.

I pull on my basketball shorts, lace up some sneakers, and get the hell out of my lonely shell of a house.

Cue the sad song.

Yep, Taylor Swift, time to call me. I'll inspire your next breakup tune.

I hit the sidewalk, lengthening my stride instantly, running hard so my mind goes as blank as it possibly can. So I can let the physical overpower the emotional.

I groan at the thought.

Emotions are not my strong suit. Hell, they're not even in my deck.

All I can do is hope a workout will rid her from my mind. That has to be what the average guy does when he gets fucked by love, right?

Trouble is, a run is what I do *to think*.

To sort through problems at work.

To find solutions.

And my brain has a brilliant idea as I finish my workout outside of Central Park. It's telling me to go talk to a friend.

But when I jog by the carousel in search of the food trucks, a long line snakes around the mint-green Luna's Sweet's vehicle. Despite my sour mood, I smile. I'm proud of my friend. I'm glad her business is thriving. And I won't disturb her with my sorry story.

I turn around, lower my shades, and make my way

out of the park, wandering past packs of cyclists speeding by and families out for Sunday afternoon picnics.

I'm half tempted to stop someone, anyone, and ask for help. Ask the harried mom wiping melted ice cream from her toddler's hand what a note like this means.

"THANKS FOR BEING MY TEACHER."

I open the text once more, hunting for a hidden meaning as I walk down Sixth Avenue, weaving among the Sunday afternoon pedestrians.

This is like a note that says: *Thank you for not smoking.* Of course I'm not smoking, and of course I was happy to be her teacher. But I don't feel like a teacher. I don't think of her as my student. She's the woman who has my heart. And I know we could be so much more. We could be everything.

But there's no business book to tell me what the hell to do when you've fallen in love with your dead best friend's sister who asked you to spend seven days seducing her. There's no *Forbes* article on how to navigate that thorny situation.

Nor is there anyone in this city of millions I want to ask.

As I turn the corner on Fifty-Fifth Street, a familiar place draws me.

The St. Regis.

I blink, almost surprised I'm here.

But not entirely.

This is one of my places.

This is an anchor, and maybe that's what I need right now.

As I head into the lobby, I picture the night with CJ. Only I'm not thinking of the stripping, though that was fantastic. I'm thinking of how we left together—as a team. How we found her brother's cat. How we packed and returned to my place and fell asleep without screwing.

My mind jumps to the next night, to dinner, when I told her I was glad I could show her what she'd been missing, and she said two simple words in reply —*me, too.*

But it wasn't the words. It was the way she said them. How she looked at me like there was more between us than just sex.

Like how it's been for me, too.

I furrow my brow as I stand in the lobby, memories from the last week crashing into me, words I didn't pay enough attention to at the time.

Before we made love. *"I'm so glad it's you."*

At the rink. *"I do trust you."*

In the town car. *"I'll miss this."*

But more than the words, I linger on the look in her eyes. Was there more hidden there all along?

I don't know the answer, but there's one person I need to talk to. I call Luna's wife.

CHAPTER 29

CJ

I find what I'm looking for at the bottom of a shoebox of cards from Sean's funeral. The church had been full of gorgeous flower arrangements, and every one of them had been accompanied by a card. I saved them all—touched by the evidence of how many people loved my brother and would miss the light he brought to the world—but I've never gone back and reread them.

It still hurts too much.

Maybe it will always hurt too much.

In my experience with grief, the weight becomes easier to carry, but I'm always aware of it, slung over my shoulder. Losing my mother so young, I'd made Death's acquaintance before I lost Sean, but never so intimately. Never with an adult's knowledge that forever without one of your special someones can be a very long time.

From the moment I open the box, freeing the scent of cardstock, long-faded flowers, and a church filled with women's perfume and musty winter coats, there are tears in my eyes.

By the time I pull out the cards and the program with Sean's smiling face on the front, two hot trails are leaking quietly down my face. But I don't fight these tears. I gave myself permission to feel this hurt a long time ago. To deny it would be to deny Sean and to push the memory of him away, which I never want to do.

I want him close, even if it hurts.

I find Graham's card near the bottom and pull it free, opening to the message written inside.

Dear CJ,

I don't know what to say.

I'm usually good with words, but they escape me now that I really need them. When I want so badly to make this easier for you, and for myself.

But I can't.

All I know is that I will never forget him. Sean was one of the best of us. He was a true friend to me, and from now on, I hope you'll let me be the same to you. I'm here for you. Anything you need. That means today, tomorrow, and ten years from now, because I'm not going anywhere.

I know I can never take his place. I wouldn't dare to try. But I'm here to hold your hand or be a shoulder to cry on or to take you for brunch the way Sean used to do. Whatever will help. I know it helps me to know that you're still here. To know I'll have someone to share memories with. I don't want to lose those memories. Or you.

Sending you all my love today, as we gather to honor your wonderful brother.

Your friend for always,
Graham

WITH MY THROAT so tight it's hard to draw a full breath, I press the card to my heart. I *knew* he had said it before. And he means it. He wants to be there for me, and the last thing I want to do is push him away.

Maybe it's time to stop moping around my apartment feeling sorry for myself and take action. To fight for Graham's heart as fiercely as I negotiated for a week in his bed.

Sure, I could sit here with my hurt feelings and try to figure out the least painful path forward. But then I would be acting like a coward, like a woman who didn't know how short life can be and how imperative it is to be brave. That may be the most important lesson I've learned, and I will draw upon all my courage to put my heart all the way on the line, no matter what. Graham is worth it, and I'm worth it, too.

"I will," I promise Sean, pressing a kiss to my finger and dropping it to his photograph. "I promise."

I box up the cards, tuck them way, then wipe my eyes. Time to be brave.

CHAPTER 30

*V*alerie opens the door to the arena for me with a stern smile and a wag of her finger. "You have five minutes."

"Thank you, Valerie."

"No, *thank you*. That Stellar Spa gift card was everything I needed. If it weren't for you, Luna would be giving me forks and paperweights." She shudders before jabbing her thumb down the hallway. "Okay, on second thought, you have ten minutes. I'll wait here for you."

I thank her for doing me a solid and letting me into the arena.

Maybe this is crazy, but it feels like the sanest thought I've had all day. Sean was my rock, the guy I turned to. He was steady, reliable, and quick with an answer. Almost always, the answer was an upbeat one. It was "seize the day" or "go for it."

And it was almost always delivered here.

This arena is where we hatched some of our greatest plans.

As I walk through the stands, closer to the ice, I swear I can feel Sean's presence. That might mean I'm losing my mind. Or maybe that's how it goes when you lose somebody you love. You can feel them in places that matter. In the things you shared.

If he were here, I'd ask him what to do next.

When you fall hard for your buddy's sister, you need to man up and let him know.

I take a seat then lower my head almost as if I'm in church, but I'm not asking God, or a saint, or even a ghost. I'm asking a friend, who happens to be on the other side.

My voice is low, barely a whisper. "I miss you, buddy. I miss you a hell of a lot. But we're doing great things, and I know you'd be proud of what we built. You'd be proud of your sister, too. She's an amazing woman, bright and beautiful and confident. She has great friends, and she knows what she wants in life."

I hope I'm part of what she wants.

I heave a sigh then say the next thing, the hardest part. But once the words are out, there's nothing tough about saying them. They are the truest words I've ever spoken.

"I didn't plan on falling in love with her. But it happened. And you know what I think? What I hope, at least? That you would tell me to go for it. Even though you'd grumble. Even though you'd threaten me with bodily injury at first, warn me never to hurt her. But in the end, I think you'd say to go for it because you'd know I'll treat her right. And I will, Sean. I will treat her like she's the most adored woman on the planet, because she is, and I don't want to lose this chance at forever."

Forever.

The word clangs in my brain.

CJ used it last night in the kitchen, while I hunted for the sushi menu.

"Do you think romance can last forever?"

I answer for myself this time.

Yes. Yes, I do. But only if you have the guts to tell the woman you want forever to be with her.

CHAPTER 31

GRAHAM

I run.

I run through the city. I cruise past couples enjoying Sunday evening dates, past families turning in after a day outside in the gorgeous spring weather. I race by guys heading to office buildings to work late on a weekend.

That's been me.

That was me just last night.

But it's not who I am now.

I run with more energy than I had when I started this morning. She's not far away, but walking is for guys who don't know they're in love.

I don't bother heading home to shower. I don't stop to buy flowers.

CJ doesn't want or need flowers. This isn't about that kind of gift. This is about something new, something different. That's what this has been about all along. She's the one. She's always been the one, never

LAUREN BLAKELY & LILI VALENTE

been far from my thoughts, even before this week together.

This time I have to go in naked, so to speak. Venture into unfamiliar territory without my usual tool kit of gifts and goodies, of lingerie and flowers. The arsenal of seduction isn't what I need right now, not tonight.

As soon as I reach her building, I run up the steps, powered by pure adrenaline and a mad need to make sure she knows I love her. I grab my phone and stab my finger against her name, calling her.

My breath comes in harsh pants as I wait for her to answer.

Her voice is shaky, a little surprised as she asks, "Hello?"

"I'm outside. I need to see you."

There's a pause. "You're . . . outside?"

Breathless, more words come. "I'm here at your apartment. I need to see you. I need to see you now, Butterfly."

Seconds later, the buzzer bleats, and I slam my hands against the door, pushing it open. I take the steps two by two up to the third floor. I turn at the landing and into her hall to find her standing in the doorway of her apartment, looking beautiful and vulnerable, and something else, too.

Hopeful.

I know the look because it's how I feel. Hope fills me up and overflows.

I don't waste time. I'm ready to give her my heart, and I pray, dirty and sweaty and empty-handed as I am, that she'll want to keep it. I close the distance to her. "I didn't give you a complete answer last night."

She lifts her chin, her gaze locking with mine. "What was the question?"

"Do I think romance can last forever?"

Her eyes widen, and she nods as if she's telling me to keep going.

"I said I didn't know because I've never felt anything like that before." I cup her cheeks. "Until you."

A sweet, small gasp escapes her lips.

"I was asleep before you. Asleep without even any decent dreams." I shake my head. "But now I'm wide awake. And the world is beautiful because I'm in love with you, CJ. I'm crazy in love with you. And I was wondering if you might possibly feel the same way?"

Her lips part, but for a long moment, she says nothing. My life, my heart, my future hang in the balance as I wait. It's probably only a few seconds, but it feels like an eternity.

The moment she finally smiles up at me, love clear in every curve of her face, is better than all her orgasms. It's her, giving me her heart to take care of.

And I will handle it with so much care.

She nods, her voice soft at first. "Yes, I *might possibly* feel the same way, Graham. I might possibly be so crazy in love with you that I've spent every moment since I left your place either in the depths of despair, or plotting ways to bring you back to me."

A weight lifts from my shoulders, banished by her words. I tug her close, needing the connection, savoring her warmth. "I thought you only wanted me for my sexy body," I say, laughing with relief.

She shakes her head with a huff. "I thought you only wanted a week, and I was so scared of losing your friendship. But then I decided I couldn't let you go without a fight. I was writing down all the reasons we're meant to be when you called."

"I like it when you fight for me." I stroke her cheek, smiling because I can't stop. "I want to read your list."

Her gaze lifts to the ceiling. "I didn't get very far. I'd just started when this guy I really like showed up on my doorstep and said he loved me."

"What a jerk that guy is," I tease.

She shakes her head, playfulness vanishing. "No, he's not a jerk. He's a wonderful man with the kindest heart and the most generous spirit, who doesn't care for emojis either, and who also happens to be *incredible* in the sack."

I laugh, grateful for the joke. It came just in time, before I started tearing up right here in the hallway.

"He taught me how good it feels to fall in love," she continues, running gentle hands up and down my back. "So good, I want to keep learning it over and over."

My heart thumps hard against my chest. "Butterfly, we'll keep learning together. You've already taught me so much more than I could ever have taught you. Turns out falling in love is pretty amazing."

She swallows hard, and her eyes shine with tears. "I'm so glad it was me."

And just like that, she reminds me again why I love her, how she opens her heart and brings me in out of the cold.

"And I'm so glad you woke me up." I dip my mouth to hers, this kiss a promise. A vow to never take her heart for granted.

Her lips brush against mine, and everything in the world feels right and true.

When we pull apart, I glance inside her place, where Stephen King is rolling around in front of the television, gnawing on her remote control. "What do you think about ditching the seven days to seduction and turning it into an always?"

"You are my always." She wiggles her eyebrows, tugs my sweaty shirt, and yanks me into her apartment. "And right now, I want all of you."

"Have me, woman," I say with a growl as the door falls shut.

In seconds, she's locked us both in her bedroom, pulled off my shirt, pushed down my shorts, and is whispering in my ear that we can do it without protection since she's on birth control.

I didn't come to her home expecting a gift, but that might be the best present of all. When I slide inside, feeling all of her, I know. I know it's only going to keep getting better.

That's another thing she's taught me, and it's a lesson I can't wait to keep learning every single day.

CHAPTER 32

GRAHAM

*I*t's Monday afternoon. Go time. The board members are gathered inside the boardroom with their beverages of choice, the glossy marketing preview our ad agency prepared, and all their preconceived notions.

Some of them want to sell.

I know that.

And I know there's a chance that *nothing* CJ or I say will change their minds.

A week ago, the thought would have turned me inside out.

But now, I have this woman, this amazing person who will be on my team—and in my heart and my bed —no matter how the vote goes today.

I'm going to be okay. Better than okay, because everything that matters is right here next to me.

"You ready?" I give her hand a quick squeeze outside the heavy brown door.

CJ looks up at me, her eyes warm and sure. "I am.

And so are you. You've got this. There's no doubt in my mind."

I grin, fighting the urge to lean down and kiss her.

Later. After the vote. I'll do it the very second we're alone, because I will need her kiss, no matter which way things go.

I swing through the door, holding it for CJ to enter before me. We take our seats as I smile at the familiar faces—even Bill and Betsy, who are wearing twin "I will not be moved" expressions. *Well, too bad, guys. I'm going to move you or die trying . . .*

Quickly, we run through the standard business matters. Then we move on to the key topic. I stand at the head of the table.

"So, as you all may know . . ." I pause, building the suspense as I take a moment to make eye contact with each person at the table. "I'm a bra man."

I'm rewarded with chuckles from most.

"Yep, I'm a bra man, a panty man, a baby doll man," I continue. "I love underwear, and I'm not afraid to admit it. I love underwear, I love women in underwear, and I love this company. Adored is more than a name to me. When Sean and I started this venture, we wanted to make sure every person who slipped into our product felt special, valued, irreplaceable. Sometimes that means they'll look in the mirror and love how a certain item of clothing makes them feel. Sometimes it means they'll blow their lover's socks off in lingerie that brings out the kind of woman they want to be."

I pace toward the window overlooking the city, motioning toward the sun-drenched skyline. "Beauty means different things to different people. Every woman out there is a unique and beautiful individual. But those women, the women who wear our lingerie, they have things in common, too. They value quality, originality, and integrity. They value themselves and believe they deserve the best."

My gaze drifts back across the room. "With our industry in a state of flux, it can be tempting to think about other options. Easier options, maybe." I shrug, lifting my hands at my sides. "Sure, why not sell our lingerie company to a conglomerate peddling everything from socks and suits to snow-cone machines and mail-order tick medicine for your dog?"

Muffled laughter assures me the room is still with me.

"But Adored has never been about easy. It's about a commitment to something fine in a world that's drowning in fast, cheap, and disposable." I meet Bill's gaze, then Betsy's, watching their expressions soften. "It's about what women deserve, not what the world has told them to settle for. You want somebody leading this company who understands that, and who understands why Adored is special. A one-company kind of man." My gaze glides briefly to CJ, enough for only her to understand as I say, "A one-woman kind of man." She smiles, making my heart do that weightless, walk-on-the-moon thing it does with her these days.

I finish with a line that is about so much more than business. "I want to be that man, and I hope you'll keep having me."

A polite smattering of applause fills the room as I motion to CJ. "Now Caroline, Sean's sister, would like to say a few words."

CJ stands, beautiful and poised as ever, and I've never been prouder to have her on my side. "Hello everyone. Believe me, I know it can be enticing to explore different options. I understand the temptation and have experienced it myself. But in the end, I realized that selling would have been a choice I made out of fear, out of a lack of belief in what I could accomplish."

Her tone gentles as she adds, "And fear is never a good reason to make a big change. If a sale was right, you would know it in your bones. It would be something you would be ready to fight for." She pauses, giving a small shake of her head. "But that's not the feeling I get here today. I sense that you all believe Adored's future is valuable, and that it should be trusted to someone who understands that."

CJ arches a wry brow as she motions my way. "And, well . . . Graham knows panties."

The laughter from the board is louder this time, but I only have eyes for this woman, this dynamite creature bringing the meeting home with a bang.

"He knows bras and bustiers and corsets." Her smile fades as she adds, "But he knows something much more important, too. He knows how to listen to women. To his customers. To the people who appreciate and value Adored's products. He listens, he learns, he adjusts, he leads—that's the hallmark of a great businessman." She glances back to me, her eyes shining. "It's also the hallmark of a great man. Thank you."

CJ sits to even louder applause, and I know we've won them over.

The vote to move forward with business as usual is

LAUREN BLAKELY & LILI VALENTE

unanimous. My company is still mine, and that makes me one happy man.

But someone else makes me even happier.

After the meeting, I steal her away, into my office, locking the door behind us.

"You were incredible," I murmur against her lips, kissing her hard and deep as I back her across the room.

"So were you." Her breath hitches as I lift her onto my desk and slide her skirt higher on her thighs. "You're sexy when you're commanding a room."

"You're sexy on my desk." I kiss a trail down her throat as I work open the buttons on her blouse. "As a matter of fact, I've had this recurring fantasy about you on my desk . . ."

Then I show her, and it's safe to say we're voting a unanimous yes to office afternoon delight.

EPILOGUE

CJ

Six weeks later . . .

THEY SAY good things come to those who wait.

I'm not sure that's always true, but I'm never going to regret waiting for Graham, this man who always knows exactly how to make me smile.

"A roller-disco, monster dress-up, twenty-sixth birthday party," I read, surveying the invitation he's submitted for my approval. I beam up at him, smiling from ear to ear. "How did you know I've always wanted to dress up like a scary clown and party all night long?"

He groans in mock dismay. "No clown. Anything but a clown."

I slide into his lap on our couch—*ours*, because I moved in with him two weeks ago, and now his home is our home—and press a kiss to his Saturday-morning scruffy cheek. "Okay, no clown. But yes. I love it. And you. And I can't wait to see you tricked out as a sexy Dracula."

He hums softly as he pulls me closer, murmuring in a terrible Transylvanian accent, "Yes, my darlink, I vill dress as Dracula and bite your beautiful body all night long."

He nips at my neck, and I dissolve into laughter that becomes a gasp and a soft moan as his kisses lose their teasing edge. We retreat to our bedroom, and he surprises me all over again with how quickly he can make me wild and ravenous, like I'm drowning in pleasure and beauty.

And afterward, once we've let a yowling Stephen King in to curl at the foot of the bed and chew on an old pair of Graham's socks—his favorite new chew toys— we snuggle and make more plans.

Plans for the Fourth of July on his friend Luna's rooftop terrace.

Plans for an August vacation to Martha's Vineyard, where we intend to eat our weight in lobster rolls.

Plans for a theater premier in September, and his birthday in October, and a visit to his parents' place in West Palm Beach in November for Thanksgiving.

Though every day feels like Thanksgiving lately.

I have so much to be grateful for.

For this man, this life, this joy, this love . . .

Graham

It RAINS every single day we're in Florida for Thanksgiving, torrential downpours that keep CJ and I locked in the house with my parents, held captive to hours of embarrassing stories from my youth, endless poker tournaments for pennies, and way too many servings of pie.

And it is unexpectedly . . . perfect.

Mom and Dad love CJ—they especially get a kick out of her *All the Fucks I Give* T-shirt she wears for luck when we're playing five-card stud—and CJ loves them. She fits in like she's slipping into an empty place in our family none of us knew was there until she stepped up.

For Christmas, my parents fly north to enjoy the holidays in the city, and I make sure to get them a hotel near all the Midtown action. We enjoy the tree in Rockefeller Center, the museums, and the Rockettes' Christmas Spectacular, and CJ and I spend our nights alone, keeping each other warm while the snow falls outside.

"Did you get everything you wanted?" I ask her as Christmas Day draws to a close and we head down the hall to bed.

"I already had everything I wanted, but yes, your gifts were perfect, as always." She presses up on tiptoe to kiss my cheek before adding in a naughty voice, "Although there is one thing I didn't find under the tree . . ."

I arch a brow, feigning ignorance, though the hand she runs over my ass leaves little doubt what my vixen has in mind. "Oh? And what's that?"

"You," she murmurs, lifting her chin. "Naked and at my mercy."

I kiss her, smiling against her lips. "That can be arranged, Butterfly. Right this very second, in fact."

And it is.

And I am—at her mercy.

When it comes to CJ, my heart is wide open, defenseless, and I wouldn't have it any other way.

ANOTHER EPILGOUE

CJ

Eleven months later...

I tug on a pretty pink sweater, fasten on one of my type-writer necklaces, then give my hair one final fluff.

Appraising my reflection in the mirror, I decide I look pretty damn good for a woman heading to Sunday morning brunch with her roommate.

Laughing at that word—as if it can even begin to encompass the depth of what we share in this home—I head to the living room, stopping to give Stephen King a scratch on the chin.

A quick purr tells me he likes the attention.

"Of course you like attention. You're a man," I say, then rub his ears. Good thing I enjoy spoiling the men in my life.

I grab my purse, sling it onto my shoulder, and I'm

scanning the room for my phone when it rings loudly from the coffee table. It's Ted, the weekend doorman.

"There's a delivery for you."

"Send it up."

A few minutes later, I answer the door and thank Ted as I take a slim white box from him. When the door shuts, I tug off the ribbon.

I furrow my brow as I find a number two pencil in it.

What on earth?

There's a note. *Bring the pencil to brunch, my butterfly.*

I shrug happily. That's Graham. He is the king of gifts, and I have to say, I love this special skill of his. Stephen King's new leather studded collar is proof that Graham can shop his butt off for anyone, or any creature.

Tucking the pencil into my purse, I head uptown to Ruby's Kitchen, where he said he'd meet me after an early morning workout. We've become regulars at Ruby's. After that first brunch when I was too shocked by the audacity of my proposal to eat, we've made it a point to rarely miss the eggs and French toast there.

Both are delish.

When I arrive, I gaze across the bowed heads of the diners, but I don't see the handsome cut of Graham's jaw, or the fantastic mess of brown hair I love to run my hands through. But I know he'll be here soon.

I tell the hostess I'm here for a party of two, and she guides me to a table right away. I take a seat, smoothing my hand over the white tablecloth, remembering the time I asked him to teach me.

That felt wild and crazy then. I would never have

expected to be back here almost a year later, tending a wonderful love that grows stronger and deeper every day.

But it does.

It most certainly does.

"Miss Murphy?"

I look up at the young face of a waiter. "Yes. Good morning."

"I have something for you." He hands me another white box, tied with a silver ribbon this time. It's bigger than the one sent to the house, about the size to hold a shirt or sweater.

Gently, I tug at the bow, letting it fall open. I reach inside to find . . .

A black composition notebook?

My brow pinches as I pick it up and read the front.

A new lesson plan.

I'm flipping it open when a voice I know well lands on my ears. "There's something I want you to teach me."

Graham stands next to me, looking as handsome as ever in jeans and a navy blue button-down, rolled up at the cuffs.

"And what would that be? How to order a double order of French toast? Because I can do that, since I'm starving." I laugh, gesturing to the chair across from me, but he remains standing. "Don't you want to sit down?"

He shakes his head. "I want to kneel."

He drops to one knee, and I gasp. My eyes turn to saucers as he opens his palm. Another box. A small, blue velvet one. "Teach me how to cherish you, to love you, and to honor you every day of our lives for as long as we both shall live."

Tears don't even have the courtesy to wait. They roll down my cheeks as he takes out a gorgeous emerald-cut diamond.

"Will you marry me?"

"Yes. Yes. Yes," I say, as he slides it onto my finger and I wrap my arms around him. "But you don't need lessons in anything. You're already perfect for me. In every single way."

Graham

Sometimes I compare my life to the movies. I turn to my favorite heroes for guidance on what they might do in a given situation. When I think of my favorite films, there's no question which one I'm starring in right now.

Every chick flick ever made.

And I couldn't be happier to picture the closing credits rolling over me as I take my seat across from the woman who's going to be my wife, and prepare to enjoy the best French toast in all of Manhattan and decades of wedded bliss.

THE END

Sign up for our newsletters to receive an alert when these sexy new books are available!

Lili Valente's newsletter: http://bit.ly/1zXpwL6

Lauren Blakely's newsletter:
Laurenblakely.com/newsletter

Coming next from Lili Valente—THE BABY MAKER, a sexy, swoony, baby-making rom com! And you won't want to MOST LIKELY TO SCORE from Lauren Blakely in January, a fun & sexy sports romance about a forbidden love. A sneak peek of each book follows.

Looking ahead to early 2018, Lauren will release WANDERLUST (hello, hot British hero) and COME AS YOU ARE!

But first, THE BABY MAKER, followed by MOST LIKELY TO SCORE...

We hope you enjoy this excerpt of
THE BABY MAKER by Lili Valente

About the Book:

Some men are troublemakers or dealmakers. The men in my family? We're baby makers.

For six generations, the women of wine country have had a saying: don't bang a Hunter man unless you want a bun in your oven.

Yeah, well. I've got a saying too: no thanks. The last

thing I need is baby makes three. My business is expanding and the only thing I'm interested in getting knocked up is my bottom line.

But then one night Emma Haverford makes me an offer I can't refuse—she backs away from the land I have my eye on in exchange for a favor…

A big, fat, baby making favor…

* * *

When I hear women have gotten pregnant shaking hands with Hunter men, I know I need Dylan Hunter's…ahem, *special skills*…way more than I need to expand my vineyard.

I'm ready to give my heart to a child and I'm tired of waiting for my late-to-the-party Prince Charming to make my dreams come true. So I promise Dylan—three months of hot, heavy, baby-making s-e-x and then I'm out of his hair forever.

But what if when it comes time to say good-bye, all I want to do is keep bottling up more memories with this big-hearted man?

This sexy Standalone romance will make you laugh, swoon, and blush baby-makin' red. Heat level: A risk of getting knocked up during download. Paperback and audio versions are especially dangerous. Handle with care...

Emma...

My gaze lifts sharply, connecting with Dylan's with an almost audible sizzle, as my heart gallops faster in my chest. It's been a while for me, but that certainly *looks* like interest of a more-than-friendly variety flickering across his features.

Time to go for it. All in. No backing down now.

I lift my chin, maintaining eye contact as I utter the six terrifying words that have been floating around my head all night, "I have a favor to ask."

"What kind of favor?"

"A big favor," I continue breathlessly, the amount of adrenaline coursing through my veins making me feel like I'm chugging uphill on a rollercoaster, headed for one hell of a drop. "But before you say no, I want to promise you that no one ever has to know about this. And when I make a promise, I keep it. Forever. I will take this secret to the grave if that's what you want. And I'll withdraw my bid on the Stroker property tomorrow so it will be yours, free and clear."

His brow furrows. "You're a confusing woman, Blondie."

"I'm sorry," I say, nibbling on my lip.

He shakes his head. "It's fine. I just thought I had an idea where you were going with that, and then you hit one into left field. So what is it you want me to do for you in exchange for withdrawing your bid?"

"I, uh…" I attempt a deeper breath, but my chest is in stress-induced lock down. No more air is getting in, so I had better use what I have left to get the words out. "I want a baby."

Dylan's brows shoot up so high and fast it would be funny if I weren't so desperate for him to agree to my plan.

"I know I could use a sperm donor," I barrel on, figuring if I'm in for a penny I might as well gamble it all. "But I don't want a stranger's baby. I want someone I know is a nice guy, and everything I've heard about you has been great. People around here love you and respect you. And I know you don't like me, but we wouldn't have to be friends. It could just be something we do for a few months to see if it works and if it doesn't, then that's fine." I wave what I hope is a breezy hand through the air. "No harm, no foul, and you still have what you want. Even if I don't get pregnant."

He makes a strangled sound that it takes me a second to realize is laughter.

"Don't laugh, please." Shame rises in my chest. "I know this may seem like it's coming out of nowhere, but I heard these two women talking today, about how the men in your family have a reputation for—"

"I know our reputation," he cuts in, sobering fast. "That's why I wrap it up. Every time. I don't want any part of that reputation. I don't want to leave a trail of

232

fatherless kids behind me, and I'm not even close to being ready to be a dad."

"I totally understand." I lift my palms into the air at my sides, showing him I have nothing to hide. "And I'm not asking you to a be a dad. I would raise the baby on my own. And maybe someday I will marry, and the baby will have a father, but I'm tired of waiting for Mr. Right to make my dreams come true. I'm running out of time. I have to make my own dreams come true, and I want to be a mother more than I've ever wanted anything. And I would be a good one. I would love that child enough to make up for not having a father in the picture, I swear I would."

"I'm sure you would." He drags a clawed hand through his hair. "But this isn't about what kind of mom you would be, Emma. It's about this being...crazy. I mean, I can't even wrap my head around it."

I swallow past the lump rising in my throat. "That's the first time you've ever said my name."

"Yeah, well, I'm sorry about that." He sounds truly apologetic. "I'm sorry I've been giving you shit and being an asshole."

"Thanks," I say, tears rising in my eyes no matter how hard I try to fight them.

"Seriously, it was nothing personal, I just... Oh God, don't cry." He reaches out, laying a warm hand on my shoulder. "Please, don't cry. There's no reason to cry."

I nod, but my face crumples anyway. "Sorry. I'm just so embarrassed. That was a hard question to ask."

"I know. I mean, I can imagine. Hell, come here." He pulls me in for a hug and I bury my face in his sweet-smelling flannel, while he runs a soothing hand up and down my back that feels so nice it makes me cry even harder.

It's been so long since someone touched me in a way that feels nice. I've been so lonely since Jeremy and I broke up. Since months before, really, when he started pulling away, distancing himself from our relationship as he started investing heavily in the bank of Jeremy and Veronica.

"It's fine," Dylan murmurs as I continue to sniffle. "You don't have to be embarrassed. We can pretend this never happened."

"Really?" I squeak.

"Absolutely. I'm good at keeping promises, too. And if I promise to forget this conversation, then it's forgotten. Word of honor. Okay?"

"Okay." I regain control as his hand shifts to a circling motion between my shoulder blades. "But I still won't be able to look you in the eye for at least six months. Maybe a year."

"Well...what if I tell you something embarrassing?" he asks after a beat. "Or at least something I would prefer you didn't know?"

I nod with my cheek still pressed against his chest, relishing the powerful feel of his body through the soft fabric, taking my comfort where I can get it since I know it will probably be a long time before I get a hug from anyone else. "Yes, please."

His hand goes still as he says, "Every time I run into you when you're wearing your glasses, I have to spend a good ten minutes fighting off inappropriate thoughts."

Surprised, I look up, but all I can see is the bottom of his chin. "What kind of inappropriate thoughts?"

He glances down. "Thoughts about how much I'd like for you to shush me at the library, then take me back to your librarian's office and let me apologize for being too loud in private."

My eyes widen, shock banishing the last of my sniffles. "You have dirty librarian fantasies about me?"

His grin is strained, embarrassed, and one of the most charming things I've ever seen. "I do. I'm sorry."

"Don't be sorry," I say, lips curving as I confess, "I've noticed how nice you look in jeans. Even before I considered the...other thing."

"Yeah, the other thing..." His focus shifts from my eyes to my mouth. "You don't want me for that job, anyway. I'm way too grouchy."

"You're grouchy during sex?" I ask, lips beginning to tingle.

His eyes darken. "No. Just in general. Could be something that's passed down in the DNA, and you don't want a grouchy kid."

"I'm okay with grouchy," I say, a ribbon of hope threading through me. "Everyone's grouchy sometimes. I just want a baby, Dylan. Grouchy or sweet, short or tall, boy or girl, I don't care." I lean into him, pulse leaping as my breasts press against his chest and his jaw clenches in response. "I know it's a lot to ask, but it wouldn't have to be weird unless we let it be weird. And I'm perfectly willing to play librarian, if that's something you're interested in."

"Now you're playing dirty, Blondie," he says, but the nickname doesn't sound teasing this time.

It sounds like a warning, a promise that if I keep

pushing something is going to give. But that's just what I want.

So I smile and say, "No, not playing dirty yet, but that can be arranged."

THE BABY MAKER is out Feb 5th!
Pre-order at www.lilivalente.com

**We hope you enjoy this preview of
MOST LIKELY TO SCORE, by Lauren Blakely.
Preorder everywhere!**

Jillian

I won't look down.

I repeat my mantra over and over, till it's branded on my brain.

This might very well be my biggest challenge, and I mastered the skill of *eyes up* many years ago.

But now? As I stand in the corner of the photo studio, I'm being tested to my limits.

I'm dying here. Simply dying.

The temptation to ogle Jones is overwhelming, and if there was ever a time to write myself a permission slip to stare now would be it. An excuse, if you will. For a second or two. That's all.

The man is posing, for crying out loud. He's the center of attention. The lights shine on his statue-of-David physique. Michelangelo would chomp at the bit to sculpt him. His body should be on display as the perfect specimen of the ideal form—carved abs with definition so fine you could scrub your sheets on his washboard; arms that could lift a woman easily and carry her up a flight of stairs before he took her; powerful thighs that suggest unparalleled stamina; and an ass that defies gravity.

I know because I've looked at his photos on many occasions. In the office. Out of the office. On my phone. On the computer.

In every freaking magazine the guy's been in.

It's my job to be aware of the press the players generate.

But it's not my job to check out his photos after hours, and I partake of that little hobby regularly. He gives my search bar quite a workout.

Still, I won't let myself stare at him in person, not in his current state of undress. My tongue would imitate a cartoon character's and slam to the floor.

If I gawk at him, I'll start crossing lines.

Lines I've mastered as a publicist for an NFL team.

It's something my mentor taught me when I began as an intern at the Renegades seven years ago, straight out of college. Lily Eckles escorted me through the locker room my first day on the job, and said, "The best piece of advice I can give you about managing your job is this: don't ever look down."

I'd furrowed my brow, trying to understand what she meant. Was it some wise, old adage, perhaps an inspirational saying about reaching for the stars?

When she opened the door to the locker room, the true meaning hit me.

Everywhere, there were dicks.

It was a parade of appendages, and swinging parts, sticks and balls as far as the eye could see.

The truth of pro ballers is simple—they let it all hang out all the time, and they love it.

So much so that the running joke among the female reporters who cover the team is that with the amount of swagger going on in the locker room when ladies are present, the TV networks should all be renamed the C&B networks.

But when you work with men who train their bodies for hours a day, and then use those same physiques to win championships, you can't be a woman who ogles them in the locker room.

ACKNOWLEDGMENTS

We are so thankful for our readers! Thank you for checking out our first ever co-written title! We hope you enjoyed reading THE V CARD as much as we enjoyed writing it. We are grateful to many people for bringing this book to you. Thank you to Helen Williams for the gorgeous cover. Huge gratitude to KP Simmon for the strategy and support on everything. Thank you to Kelley, Candi and Keyanna for the day to day work that is so vital.

On the editorial side, thank you to Lauren Clarke, Virginia, Tiffany, Karen, and Janice for their keen eyes.

Huge love and forever hugs to our families, who know the proper care and feeding of a romance writer, and in this case, a pair!

Most of all, we are thankful every day for our readers.

DEEP DOMINATION

DESPERATE DOMINATION

DIVINE DOMINATION

Kidnapped by the Billionaire Series—HOT novellas, must be read in order.

FILTHY WICKED LOVE

CRAZY BEAUTIFUL LOVE

ONE MORE SHAMELESS NIGHT

Under His Command Series—HOT novellas, must be read in order.

CONTROLLING HER PLEASURE

COMMANDING HER TRUST

CLAIMING HER HEART

To the Bone Series—Sexy Romantic Suspense, must be read in order.

A LOVE SO DANGEROUS

A LOVE SO DEADLY

A LOVE SO DEEP

Fight for You Series—Emotional New Adult Romantic Suspense. Read in order.

RUN WITH ME

FIGHT FOR YOU

Bedding The Bad Boy Series—must be read in order.

THE BAD BOY'S TEMPTATION

THE BAD BOY'S SEDUCTION

THE BAD BOY'S REDEMPTION

The Lonesome Point Series—Sexy Cowboys written with Jessie Evans.

LEATHER AND LACE

SADDLES AND SIN

DIAMONDS AND DUST

12 DATES OF CHRISTMAS

GLITTER AND GRIT

SUNNY WITH A CHANCE OF TRUE LOVE

CHAPS AND CHANCE

ROPES AND REVENGE

8 SECOND ANGEL

Sweet Sinful Nights, Sinful Desire, Sinful Longing and Sinful Love, the complete New York Times Bestselling high-heat romantic suspense series that spins off from Seductive Nights!

Playing With Her Heart, a USA Today bestseller, and a sexy Seductive Nights spin-off standalone! (Davis and Jill's romance)

21 Stolen Kisses, the USA Today Bestselling forbidden new adult romance!

Caught Up In Us, a New York Times and USA Today Bestseller! (Kat and Bryan's romance!)

Pretending He's Mine, a Barnes & Noble and iBooks Bestseller! (Reeve & Sutton's romance)

Trophy Husband, a New York Times and USA Today Bestseller! (Chris & McKenna's romance)

Far Too Tempting, the USA Today Bestselling standalone romance! (Matthew and Jane's romance)

Stars in Their Eyes, an iBooks bestseller! (William and Jess' romance)

My USA Today bestselling No Regrets series that includes

The Thrill of It (Meet Harley and Trey)

and its sequel

Every Second With You

My New York Times and USA Today Bestselling Fighting Fire series that includes

Burn For Me (Smith and Jamie's romance!)

Melt for Him (Megan and Becker's romance!)

and *Consumed by You* (Travis and Cara's romance!)

The Sapphire Affair series...

The Sapphire Affair

The Sapphire Heist

Out of Bounds

A New York Times Bestselling sexy sports romance

The Only One

A second chance love story!

CONTACT

We love hearing from readers! You can find Lauren on Twitter at LaurenBlakely3, Facebook at LaurenBlakelyBooks, Instagram at LaurenBlakelyBooks, or online at LaurenBlakely.com. You can also email Lauren at laurenblakelybooks@gmail.com

Find Lili on Twitter at lili_valente_ro, Facebook at AuthorLiliValente, or online at LiliValente.com. You can also email Lili at lili.valente.romancc@gmail.com.